# 高一同學的目標

1.「用會話背7000字①」書 + CD 280元

以三個極短句為一組的方式,讓同學背了會話,同時快速增加單字。高一同學要從「國中常用2000字」挑戰「高中常用7000字」,加強單字是第一目標。

2.「一分鐘背9個單字」書 + CD 280元

利用字首、字尾的排列,讓
1個字簡單。

*3. rival*

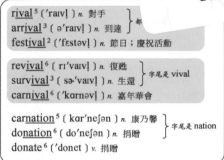

rival⁵ ('raɪvḷ ) n. 對手
arrival³ ( ə'raɪvḷ ) n. 到達　都
festival² ('fɛstəvḷ ) n. 節日;慶祝活動

revival⁶ ( rɪ'vaɪvḷ ) n. 復甦
survival³ ( sə'vaɪvḷ ) n. 生還　字尾是 vival
carnival⁶ ('karnəvḷ ) n. 嘉年華會

carnation⁵ ( kar'neʃən ) n. 康乃馨
donation⁶ ( do'neʃən ) n. 捐贈　字尾是 nation
donate⁶ ('donet ) v. 捐贈

3.「一口氣考試英語」書 + CD 280元

把大學入學考試題目編成會話,背了以後,會說英語,又會考試。

例如:

What a nice surprise! (真令人驚喜!)【常考】
I can't believe my eyes.
(我無法相信我的眼睛。)
*Little did I dream of seeing you here.*
(做夢也沒想到會在這裡看到你。)【駒澤大】

4.「一口氣背文法」書＋CD  280元
  英文文法範圍無限大，規則無限多，誰背得完？
  劉毅老師把文法整體的概念，編成216句，背完
  了會做文法題、會說英語，也會寫作文。既是一
  本文法書，也是一本會話書。

### 1. 現在簡單式的用法

| | |
|---|---|
| I *get up* early every day. | 我每天早起。 |
| I *understand* this rule now. | 我現在了解這條規定了。 |
| Actions *speak* louder than words. | 行動勝於言辭。 |

【二、三句強調實踐早起】

5.「高中英語聽力測驗①」書＋MP3  280元

6.「高中英語聽力測驗進階」書＋MP3  280元
  高一月期考聽力佔20％，我們根據大考中心公布的
  聽力題型編輯而成。

7.「高一月期考英文試題」書  280元
  收集建中、北一女、師大附中、中山、成功、景
  美女中等各校試題，並聘請各校名師編寫模擬試
  題。

8.「高一英文克漏字測驗」書  180元

9.「高一英文閱讀測驗」書  180元
  全部取材自高一月期考試題，英雄
  所見略同，重複出現的機率很高。
  附有翻譯及詳解，不必查字典，對
  錯答案都有明確交待，做完題目，
  一看就懂。

# 高二同學的目標——提早準備考大學

## 1.「用會話背7000字①②」
書+CD，每冊280元

「用會話背7000字」能夠解決所有學英文的困難。高二同學可先從第一冊開始背，第一冊和第二冊沒有程度上的差異，背得越多，單字量越多，在腦海中的短句越多。每一個極短句大多不超過5個字，1個字或2個字都可以成一個句子，如：「用會話背7000字①」p.184，每一句都2個字，好背得不得了，而且與生活息息相關，是每個人都必須知道的知識，例如：成功的祕訣是什麼？

### *11. What are the keys to success?*

| | |
|---|---|
| Be *ambitious*. | 要有<u>雄</u>心。 |
| Be *confident*. | 要有<u>信</u>心。 |
| Have *determination*. | 要有<u>決</u>心。 |
| | |
| Be *patient*. | 要有<u>耐</u>心。 |
| Be *persistent*. | 要有<u>恆</u>心。 |
| Show *sincerity*. | 要有<u>誠</u>心。 |
| | |
| Be *charitable*. | 要有<u>愛</u>心。 |
| Be *modest*. | 要<u>虛</u>心。 |
| Have *devotion*. | 要<u>專</u>心。 |

當你背單字的時候，就要有「雄心」，要「決心」背好，對自己要有「信心」，一定要有「耐心」和「恆心」，背書時要「專心」。

背完後，腦中有2,160個句子，那不得了，無限多的排列組合，可以寫作文。有了單字，翻譯、閱讀測驗、克漏字都難不倒你了。高二的時候，要下定決心，把7000字背熟、背爛。雖然高中課本以7000字為範圍，編書者為了便宜行事，往往超出7000字，同學背了少用的單字，反倒忽略真正重要的單字。千萬記住，背就要背「高中常用7000字」，背完之後，天不怕、地不怕，任何考試都難不倒你。

2. 「時速破百單字快速記憶」書 250 元

**字尾是 try，重音在倒數第三音節上**

entry³ (ˈɛntrɪ) *n.* 進入【No entry. 禁止進入。】
country¹ (ˈkʌntrɪ) *n.* 國家；鄉下【ou 讀 /ʌ/，為例外字】
ministry⁴ (ˈmɪnɪstrɪ) *n.* 部【mini = small】

chemistry⁴ (ˈkɛmɪstrɪ) *n.* 化學
geometry⁵ (dʒɪˈɑmətrɪ) *n.* 幾何學【geo 土地，metry 測量】
industry² (ˈɪndəstrɪ) *n.* 工業；勤勉【這個字重音常唸錯】

poetry¹ (ˈpo·ɪtrɪ) *n.* 詩
poultry⁴ (ˈpoltrɪ) *n.* 家禽 ⎫
pastry⁵ (ˈpestrɪ) *n.* 糕餅 ⎭ 字尾 y 表「集合名詞」

3. 「高二英文克漏字測驗」書 180 元

4. 「高二英文閱讀測驗」書 180 元
全部選自各校高二月期考試題精華，英雄所見略同，再出現的機率很高。

5. 「7000字學測試題詳解」書 250 元
一般模考題為了便宜行事，往往超出7000字範圍，無論做多少份試題，仍然有大量生字，無法進步。唯有鎖定7000字為範圍的試題，才會對準備考試有幫助。每份試題都經「劉毅英文」同學實際考過，效果奇佳。附有詳細解答，單字標明級數，對錯答案都有明確交待，不需要再查字典，做完題目，再看詳解，快樂無比。

6. 「高中常用7000字解析【豪華版】」書 390 元
按照「大考中心高中英文參考詞彙表」編輯而成。難背的單字有「記憶技巧」、「同義字」及「反義字」，關鍵的單字有「典型考題」。大學入學考試核心單字，以紅色標記。

7. 「高中7000字測驗題庫」書 180 元
取材自大規模考試，解答詳盡，節省查字典的時間。

## 編者的話

　　英文作文是大學入試必考的題型，且佔分高達 **20** 分，其重要性自不待言。而考試時間緊迫，同學必須在最短的時間內，寫出一篇通順達意且文法正確的英文作文，所以平時就應累積實力，**多看、多背各類型的範文**，應考時才能文思泉湧、左右逢源，締造佳績。

　　針對同學的需要，我們依據大學學測及指考英文作文的命題趨勢，精選 **100** 個最熱門的題目，以中國學生的思想觀念為主，由外國老師執筆，彙編成「**易背英作文 100 篇**」（*100 English Compositions for the College Entrance Exam*）。

　　本書的範文簡短易背，研讀時可配合流暢的翻譯與詳盡的註解，不僅能節省查字典的時間，也可以在無形中充實字彙與文法的能力、磨練中英對譯的技巧，可收一舉數得、事半功倍之效。

　　審慎的編校是我們一貫堅持的原則，倘有疏漏之處，請各界先進不吝批評指教，使本書更臻於盡善盡美之境。

編者　謹識

# 易背英作文100篇

## 100 English Compositions
## for the College Entrance Exam

# CONTENTS

✎ 經 驗 ·········

👁 看法 .........

 環 境

科技・交通

# 1. My Father

My father is the greatest man that I have ever met. He is a lawyer, and he always appears to be calm and fair. *For example*, when I have arguments with my brother, my father always settles them fairly. He comes up with a judgment acceptable to both of us; *at the same time*, he also shows us what justice is. Because of his influence, I have decided to be a lawyer in the future.

My father is also a good friend. He is always willing to give me the best advice. When I turn to him for help, he shows me the way to solve the problems and guides me through my bad moods. Besides asking for help, I also share my happiness with him. Sometimes I even tell him some secrets that are only told between friends. *My father is not only a good parent but also my best friend*.

# 1. 我的父親

　　我的父親是我所見過最偉大的人。他是一位律師，似乎總是非常的冷靜而且公正。例如，當我和弟弟吵架時，父親總會公平地解決我們的紛爭。他會提出一個我和弟弟都能接受的裁決；同時，他也會告訴我們，怎麼樣才算公平。由於父親的影響，我已經決定以後也要當一名律師。

　　父親也是我的好朋友。他總是樂於提供最好的建議給我。當我向他求助時，他會告訴我問題的解決之道，引導我，使我心情不再低落。除了找他幫忙之外，我也會和他一起分享我的喜悅。有時我甚至會告訴他一些只有朋友之間才會說的秘密。他不僅是個好父親，也是我最好的朋友。

**

calm〔kɑm〕*adj.* 冷靜的　　fair〔fɛr〕*adj.* 公平的
argument〔'ɑrgjəmənt〕*n.* 爭論
settle〔'sɛtḷ〕*v.* 解決　　***come up with*** 提出；想出
judgment〔'dʒʌdʒmənt〕*n.* 裁決；判決
acceptable〔 ək'sɛptəbḷ〕*adj.* 可接受的
justice〔'dʒʌstɪs〕*n.* 公平；公正
influence〔'ɪnfluəns〕*n.* 影響
willing〔'wɪlɪŋ〕*adj.* 願意的
***turn to*** *sb.* ***for help*** 向某人求助
guide〔gaɪd〕*v.* 引導　　mood〔mud〕*n.* 心情
***not only…but also*** ~ 不僅…，而且~

# 2. My Goal in Life

*Life without a goal is like sailing on the sea without a destination. Not knowing where to go, we can only linger at the crossroads of life.* Having a goal which we believe in gives us direction, stability, and the chance for fulfillment.

Being a teacher has long been my goal in life. It is a noble and professional job which requires great affection, patience, and dedication. It is also a challenging job since the teacher is faced with students of many different aptitudes. I am sure that I will have a very good experience while teaching and I consider it a good goal.

# 2. 我的人生目標

人生沒有目標，就如同在沒有目的地的茫茫大海中航行。如果不知道何去何從，我們就只能徘徊在人生的十字路口。有一個堅信不移的目標，生活便更有方向、更具穩定性，並且有機會實現我們的目標。

長久以來，當老師一直是我的人生目標。老師是種既崇高又專業的工作，必須有極大的愛心、耐心，以及犧牲奉獻的精神。老師必須面對許多不同程度的學生，所以是具有挑戰性的工作。我相信在教學期間，一定能獲得很好的經驗，因此我認為當老師是個很好的目標。

**\*\***

goal〔gol〕*n.* 目標　　sail〔sel〕*v.* 航行
destination〔͵dɛstə'neʃən〕*n.* 目的地
linger〔'lɪŋgɚ〕*v.* 徘徊
crossroads〔'krɔs͵rodz〕*n.* 十字路口
stability〔stə'bɪlətɪ〕*n.* 穩定性
fulfillment〔fʊl'fɪlmənt〕*n.* 實現
noble〔'nobḷ〕*adj.* 崇高的；高尚的
affection〔ə'fɛkʃən〕*n.* 感情；愛
dedication〔͵dɛdə'keʃən〕*n.* 奉獻
challenging〔'tʃælɪndʒɪŋ〕*adj.* 有挑戰性的
***be faced with*** 面對（＝*face*）
aptitude〔'æptə͵tjud〕*n.* 能力

## 3. My Hobby

*Hobbies can increase the enjoyment of our lives.* We can gain much pleasure by spending time on them. *On the contrary*, if we waste our time, for example, drinking and gambling, we not only spoil our lives, but also cause much trouble to others. *Therefore*, it is always a good idea to cultivate a good hobby.

Playing the harmonica has been my hobby for a long time. Whenever I have spare time, I play the harmonica, either for the fun of it, or, if I am in a bad mood, to lift my spirits. I regard it as worthwhile to spend my time playing the harmonica, and I will never give up this hobby.

# 3. 我的嗜好

　　嗜好可以增加我們的生活樂趣。做自己喜歡的事，能獲得很大的樂趣。相反地，如果我們浪費時間，例如把時間花在喝酒或賭博，不僅會破壞我們的生活，還會對別人造成很多的困擾。因此，培養良好的嗜好是個很好的想法。

　　長久以來，吹口琴一直是我的嗜好。當我有空時，就會吹口琴，有時只是爲了好玩，有時當我心情不好時，吹口琴可以振奮我的精神。我認爲花時間吹口琴是十分值得的，所以我永遠都不會放棄這項嗜好。

** ─────────────────────

enjoyment〔ɪnˈdʒɔɪmənt〕*n.* 快樂；喜悅
gain〔gen〕*v.* 獲得　　***on the contrary*** 相反地
gamble〔ˈgæmbl̩〕*v.* 賭博
***not only…but also*** ~ 不僅…，而且~
trouble〔ˈtrʌbl̩〕*n.* 麻煩；困擾
cultivate〔ˈkʌltəˌvet〕*v.* 培養
harmonica〔harˈmɑnɪkə〕*n.* 口琴
***spare time*** 空閒時間　　mood〔mud〕*n.* 心情
lift〔lɪft〕*v.* 提升　　spirit〔ˈspɪrɪt〕*n.* 精神
worthwhile〔ˈwɜθˈhwaɪl〕*adj.* 值得做的
***give up*** 放棄

# 4. My Hometown

My hometown is in the beautiful county of Ilan in northeastern Taiwan. Surrounded by mountains, Ilan has little traffic and has not been spoiled by swarms of visitors. Ilan is clean and quiet and claims to have the purest water on the island as its rivers are less polluted. *It is a place of scenic beauty with green fields, mountains and rivers*.

Ilan is also dear to me because of the many memories associated with it. I can never forget my childhood playmates and all our games. We used to chase each other in the fields, climb trees and play in the grass. Thinking of this makes me smile. *I will never forget the wonderful memories of my youth*.

# 4. 我的故鄉

　　我的故鄉是位於台灣東北部美麗的宜蘭縣。由於群山環繞，宜蘭的交通流量小，因此能免於大批遊客所帶來的破壞。宜蘭地區乾淨而且十分寧靜，由於河川較少受到污染，所以水質可算是全省最潔淨的。宜蘭有翠綠的田野、山林與河川，風景相當優美。

　　宜蘭也是我心愛的地方，因為我有許多關於宜蘭的回憶。我永遠都無法忘記兒時的玩伴和遊戲。我們以前常在田野中互相追逐、爬樹，並且在草地上遊玩。每當想起這些往事，總會令我微笑。我會永遠記得這些年輕時美好的回憶。

**

county〔'kauntɪ〕*n.* 縣
northeastern〔ˌnɔrθ'istən〕*adj.* 東北的
surround〔sə'raund〕*v.* 環繞
spoil〔spɔɪl〕*v.* 破壞
swarm〔swɔrm〕*n.* (人、動物的) 群；群眾；大批
claim〔klem〕*v.* 宣稱　　　pure〔pjur〕*adj.* 潔淨的
scenic〔'sinɪk〕*adj.* 風景的　　dear〔dɪr〕*adj.* 心愛的
associate〔ə'soʃɪˌet〕*v.* 與～有關
playmate〔'pleˌmet〕*n.* 玩伴　　***used to*** 以前
chase〔tʃes〕*v.* 追逐　　grass〔græs〕*n.* 草地
youth〔juθ〕*n.* 年輕的時候

# 5. My Method of Studying

*Studying without a method is like traveling in the mountains without a compass.* Not knowing the right direction, you may waste much time trying every possible way and still fail to reach your goal. *Likewise*, studying without organization wastes time and is ineffective. It is therefore essential to identify what it is we want to achieve, and to organize a plan.

I have developed a method of studying which emphasizes staying alert and constant review. Being attentive in class or while reading enables me to comprehend and memorize materials easily and quickly. I also prefer to study at night, especially after everyone has gone to bed. The peace and quiet allow me to concentrate on my reading.

# 5. 我的讀書方法

　　讀書沒有方法，就像在山區旅行沒帶指南針一樣。如果不知道正確的方向，可能會浪費許多時間嘗試每一種可能的方法，卻仍然無法達到目標。同樣地，讀書沒有計劃，既浪費時間也沒有成效。因此，認清我們所要達成的目標，再擬定計劃，是十分必要的。

　　我已經研發出一套讀書方法，重點在於集中注意力，而且要不斷地複習。上課或唸書時專心的話，使我能夠輕易又迅速地理解和記憶。我也比較喜歡在晚上唸書，特別是當大家都上床睡覺以後。周遭寂靜無聲，能讓我唸書時更專心。

**

compass〔ˈkʌmpəs〕*n.* 羅盤；指南針
*fail to V.* 無法～　　likewise〔ˈlaɪkˌwaɪz〕*adv.* 同樣地
ineffective〔ˌɪnəˈfɛktɪv〕*adj.* 無效的
essential〔əˈsɛnʃəl〕*adj.* 必要的
identify〔aɪˈdɛntəˌfaɪ〕*v.* 認清　　achieve〔əˈtʃiv〕*v.* 達到
organize〔ˈɔrɡənˌaɪz〕*v.* 組織；籌劃
develop〔dɪˈvɛləp〕*v.* 研發
alert〔əˈlɝt〕*adj.* 警覺的；注意的
constant〔ˈkɑnstənt〕*adj.* 不斷的
review〔rɪˈvju〕*n.* 複習　　attentive〔əˈtɛntɪv〕*adj.* 注意的
comprehend〔ˌkɑmprɪˈhɛnd〕*v.* 理解
memorize〔ˈmɛməˌraɪz〕*v.* 背誦；記憶
*peace and quiet* 安靜　　*concentrate on* 專心於

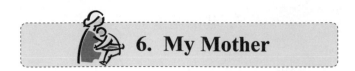

# 6. My Mother

My mother is like a great magician. She can do many impossible things. In the kitchen, she performs magic on all kinds of food. She can turn plain food into the most delicious food I have ever tasted. When it comes to household chores, my mother is able to clean the living room and wash the floor within minutes. ***Therefore***, she seems so great and incredible to me.

My mother did not receive much education, but she encourages me to continue with my studies. When I am tired of reading boring textbooks, my mother always comes to comfort me and keep me company. Sometimes, when I stay up late, she either prepares some snacks for me or stays up with me. ***Thanks to her patience and dedication, I have the perseverance to go on***.

# 6. 我的母親

　　我的母親像是一位很棒的魔術師。她能做許多不可思議的事。在廚房裏,她會對各種的食物施魔法。她能把最普通的食物,變成我所吃過最好吃的食物。至於做家事,我母親可以在幾分鐘之內,把客廳打掃乾淨,並清洗地板。因此,對我而言,她非常屬害,而且不可思議。

　　我母親並沒有受過很多教育,但她卻鼓勵我繼續讀書。當我因閱讀無聊的教科書而覺得厭煩時,母親總會來安慰我,並陪在我身邊。有時當我熬夜到很晚,她會為我準備一些點心,或是陪我一起熬夜。由於母親的犧牲奉獻與耐心,我才能有毅力繼續向前邁進。

**

magician〔məˋdʒɪʃən〕 *n.* 魔術師
perform〔pɚˋfɔrm〕 *v.* 施行
magic〔ˋmædʒɪk〕 *n.* 魔法　　***turn A into B*** 把 A 變成 B
plain〔plen〕 *adj.* 平凡的　　***when it comes to*** 一提到
household〔ˋhaʊsˏhold〕 *adj.* 家庭的
chores〔tʃɔrz〕 *n. pl.* 雜事
***household chores*** 家事 ( = *housework* )
incredible〔ɪnˋkrɛdəbḷ〕 *adj.* 不可思議的
***be tired of*** 厭倦　　comfort〔ˋkʌmfɚt〕 *v.* 安慰
***keep sb. company*** 陪伴某人
snack〔snæk〕 *n.* 零食;點心　　***thanks to*** 因為;由於
dedication〔ˏdɛdəˋkeʃən〕 *n.* 奉獻
perseverance〔ˏpɝsəˋvɪrəns〕 *n.* 毅力

# 7. My Motto

In front of my desk is a motto which was given to me by my father years ago. It is "***Look before you leap***." Seeing it always reminds me of why I got this motto. At the age of thirteen, I was too young to think thoroughly and carefully. Misled by bad friends, I was rebellious and against everything.

***One day***, my father wrote another motto for me. He wrote that I should stop being so selfish and try to be considerate to others. When I'm about to do something, I should ponder it for a while, thinking about whether it would hurt someone or not. With careful thought, I will not make impulsive mistakes. I have benefited a lot from my father's teaching. ***Now I always think carefully before taking action lest I should do something wrong***.

# 7. 我的座右銘

　　我的書桌前，有一句父親好幾年前送給我的座右銘，那就是「三思而後行」。看到這句話，就會使我想起得到這句座右銘的原因。十三歲時，我年紀還太小，不會全面、而且仔細地思考事情。由於壞朋友的誤導，我變得很叛逆，任何事都想反抗。

　　有一天，我的父親寫了另一句座右銘給我。他寫說我不應該這麼自私，必須多為別人著想。做事之前，要仔細考慮一下，想想看是不是會傷害到別人。如果能仔細思考，我就不會因為一時的衝動而犯錯。父親的教誨使我獲益良多。現在每當我要採取行動之前，為了避免做錯事，我都會謹慎地思考。

**\*\***

motto〔'mɑto〕*n.* 座右銘　　leap〔lip〕*v.* 跳
***Look before you leap.*** 【諺】三思而行。
thoroughly〔'θʒolɪ〕*adv.* 完全地；徹底地
mislead〔mɪs'lid〕*v.* 誤導
rebellious〔rɪ'bɛljəs〕*adj.* 反叛的
against〔ə'gɛnst〕*prep.* 反對
selfish〔'sɛlfɪʃ〕*adj.* 自私的
considerate〔kən'sɪdərɪt〕*adj.* 體貼的
ponder〔'pɑndɚ〕*v.* 沈思；考慮
impulsive〔ɪm'pʌlsɪv〕*adj.* 衝動的
benefit〔'bɛnəfɪt〕*v.* 獲益
***take action*** 採取行動　　lest〔lɛst〕*conj.* 以免

## 8. My Pet

My pet was a beautiful dog which was given to me by my father on my eleventh birthday. It was a pretty white dog with short legs and long hair. ***Not having any brothers or sisters, I came to see the dog as a brother and a playmate.*** Every day when I came home from school, I would spend the whole afternoon playing with it.

***One day*** when I got home from school it did not show up at the door. My mother explained that it had been summoned to be an angel in heaven. Old enough to know what this meant, I cried over the news and refused to believe the truth. For a long time, I felt terrible at the thought of my dog. But when my father suggested giving me another dog, I refused, because nothing could ever take the place of my dog.

# 8. 我的寵物

我的寵物是隻漂亮的小狗，是我十一歲生日時，父親送給我的禮物。牠是隻漂亮的白狗，有著長長的毛、短短的腿。由於我沒有兄弟姐妹，所以就把這隻小狗當作是我的兄弟兼玩伴。每天放學回家的時候，我會跟牠玩一整個下午。

有一天，當我放學回家時，牠並沒有出現在門口。母親向我解釋說，牠已經蒙主寵召，到天堂當天使了。我年紀已經不小，知道這是什麼意思，這個消息令我哭得十分傷心，拒絕相信這是事實。有好長一段時間，每當想起我的狗，我心情就變得很糟。但是當父親提議要送我另一隻狗時，我拒絕了，因為沒有任何東西能取代我的狗。

**\*\***

pet〔pɛt〕*n.* 寵物　　pretty〔ˋprɪtɪ〕*adj.* 漂亮的
hair〔hɛr〕*n.* 毛；頭髮　　*come to* 開始
*see* A *as* B 視 A 為 B　　playmate〔ˋpleˏmet〕*n.* 玩伴
*show up* 出現　　summon〔ˋsʌmən〕*v.* 召喚
angel〔ˋendʒəl〕*n.* 天使　　heaven〔ˋhɛvən〕*n.* 天堂
*at the thought of* 一想到　　refuse〔rɪˋfjuz〕*v.* 拒絕
ever〔ˋɛvɚ〕*adv.* 有；會；在任何時候
*take the place of* 代替

# 9. My School Life

Tests! Tests! Tests! *Taking tests is the burden of every senior high school student*. My life is filled with homework and tests instead of playing and dreaming. *In the morning*, I typically rush to school for a morning quiz; *at night*, I stay up late for the next day's exams. *Day after day*, I repeat the same boring life.

My only pleasure is to take a walk with my friends during the ten-minute school breaks. While walking, we discuss things or just sing song after song instead of talking. Although the ten minutes passes quickly, we are always refreshed by this break. These breaks are the only thing that help me get through class after class.

# 9. 我的學校生活

　　考試！考試！考試！參加考試對每個高中生而言，是個沈重的負擔。我的生活都被作業與考試填滿了，沒空玩樂與做夢。早上我通常必須趕到學校去參加小考；而晚上，則必須熬夜準備隔天的考試。我就這樣，日復一日地重覆著同樣無聊的生活。

　　我唯一的樂趣，就是利用學校十分鐘的休息時間，和朋友一起去散散步。散步的時候，我們會討論事情，或是一首接一首地唱歌，而不交談。儘管十分鐘很快就過去了，但經過這樣的休息之後，我們的精神總是很快就能恢復。就是這些片刻的休息時間，使我能夠一堂接一堂地上完每一節課。

*****————————————————

***take a test*** 參加考試　　burden〔'bɝdn̩〕*n.* 負擔
***be filled with*** 充滿了　　***instead of*** 而不是
rush〔rʌʃ〕*v.* 衝　　typically〔'tɪpɪklɪ〕*adv.* 通常
quiz〔kwɪz〕*n.* 小考　　***stay up*** 熬夜
***day after day*** 一天又一天
repeat〔rɪ'pit〕*v.* 重覆　　***take a walk*** 散步
break〔brek〕*n.* 休息時間
refresh〔rɪ'frɛʃ〕*v.* 使恢復精神
***get through*** 度過

# 10. My Weakness

*No one is perfect, and I am no exception. Napoleon once declared that "Victory belongs to the most persevering."* Lack of perseverance is my biggest weakness. I often give up easily. *Sometimes* I begin things with great enthusiasm, but end up discouraged. *In other cases* I postpone things or lack the patience to continue my work. Often I prevent myself from being successful.

To correct my weakness, I am determined to be more patient. Patience will allow me to concentrate better, and not give up so easily. *From patience and hard work will come a greater chance of success.*

# 10. 我的缺點

　　沒有人是完美的，我也不例外。拿破崙曾宣稱：
「勝利是屬於最不屈不撓的人。」缺乏毅力是我最大的
缺點。我常常很容易就放棄。我有時做事情，剛開始會
很有熱忱，但到最後便會氣餒。在其他情況，我也常拖
延事情，或缺乏耐心繼續完成我的工作，所以常常無法
成功。

　　為了要改正我的缺點，我下定決心要更有耐心。耐
心能使我更專心，不會那麼容易就放棄。有耐心，並且
肯努力的話，就比較有機會能成功。

**

weakness〔'wiknɪs〕*n.* 缺點
Napoleon〔nə'poljən〕*n.* 拿破崙
declare〔dɪ'klɛr〕*v.* 宣稱
victory〔'vɪktərɪ〕*n.* 勝利
persevering〔͵pɝsə'vɪrɪŋ〕*adj.* 不屈不撓的
lack〔læk〕*n.* 缺乏
perseverance〔͵pɝsə'vɪrəns〕*n.* 毅力
enthusiasm〔ɪn'θjuzɪ͵æzəm〕*n.* 熱忱
***end up*** 最後…
discouraged〔dɪs'kɝɪdʒd〕*adj.* 氣餒的
case〔kes〕*n.* 情況
postpone〔post'pon〕*v.* 拖延
***prevent sb. from V-ing*** 使某人無法～
***be determined to*** 決心　　come〔kʌm〕*v.* 產生

# 11. My Favorite Book

My favorite book is the romance novel "Gone with the Wind ". In the novel, a young woman, Scarlett O'Hara, tells everyone that she is in love with a man named Ashley Wilkes. But there is another man, Rhett Butler, who has a powerful effect on her, and it is not until Rhett decides to leave that Scarlett realizes who she truly loves. The book is about truth and imagination. What we believe we are is not necessarily what we really are.

In addition to the love story, I also appreciate the philosophy of Scarlett. For her, "*Tomorrow is another day.*" *When I am in a low mood, I always tell myself that tomorrow will be a better day*. Reading "Gone with the Wind " is not only enjoyable, but also a good reminder of this truth about tomorrow.

# 11. 我最喜歡的書

我最喜歡的書，就是愛情小說
「飄」。在書中，有位名叫郝思嘉的
年輕女子，告訴大家她愛的是一個叫
衛希禮的男人。但另一個男人白瑞德，
卻對她有著強烈的影響，直到白瑞德決定要離開時，郝
思嘉才知道自己真正愛的是誰。這本書是關於事實與想
像之間的差異。我們對自己的看法，未必完全正確。

除了愛情故事之外，我也很欣賞郝思嘉的人生觀。
對她而言，「明天又是嶄新的一天。」當我心情不好的
時候，我總是告訴自己，明天會更好。讀「飄」這本書，
不僅使我很愉快，也提醒我要對「明天」有更正確的看
法。

**

romance〔roˋmæns〕*n.* 愛情故事
powerful〔ˋpauəfəl〕*adj.* 強大的
effect〔ɪˋfɛkt〕*n.* 影響（= *influence*）
***it is not until…that~*** 直到…才~
***not necessarily*** 未必（= *not always*）
appreciate〔əˋpriʃɪ͵et〕*v.* 欣賞
philosophy〔fəˋlasəfɪ〕*n.* 哲學；人生觀
enjoyable〔ɪnˋdʒɔɪəbḷ〕*adj.* 令人愉快的
reminder〔rɪˋmaɪndɚ〕*n.* 提醒的人或物

# 12. My Favorite Festival

***The Chinese New Year is the most important festival of all, and it is my favorite, too.*** It is a vacation when Chinese gather together. Children studying abroad, travelers sightseeing in foreign countries, and busy workers working far away from home all rush back to their hometowns.

There is a series of celebrations during Chinese New Year. On Chinese New Year's Eve, the family members reunite and enjoy a square meal. After the meal comes the happiest moment for children, because they can receive red envelopes with money inside. During Chinese New Year, people go outdoors and keep saying "Congratulations!" when they meet people, even if they are strangers   The celebrations continue for a long time, and people make wishes for a prosperous year.

# 12. 我最喜歡的節日

農曆新年是所有節日中最重要的,也是我最喜歡的節日。農曆新年假期是中國人闔家團圓的時刻。出國唸書的孩子、到外國觀光的遊客,以及遠離家鄉工作十分忙碌的人,全部都會趕回故鄉。

在農曆新年期間,會有一系列的慶祝活動。在除夕夜,一家人會團聚,一起享用豐盛的晚餐。吃完晚餐後,就到了孩子們最快樂的時刻,因為他們可以收到裝有壓歲錢的紅包。農曆新年期間,大家出門遇到人時,即使是遇見陌生人,也會互道「恭禧!」。慶祝活動會持續很久,而人們也會許下願望,希望能有個順遂的一年。

** ————————————————

festival〔ˈfɛstəvḷ〕*n.* 節日
gather〔ˈɡæðɚ〕*v.* 聚集
abroad〔əˈbrɔd〕*adv.* 在國外
sightsee〔ˈsaɪtˌsi〕*v.* 觀光
***rush back to*** 急忙回到　　***a series of*** 一系列的
reunite〔ˌrijuˈnaɪt〕*v.* 團聚
square〔skwɛr〕*adj.* 豐盛的;充實的
***red envelope*** 紅包　　***make a wish*** 許願
prosperous〔ˈprɑspərəs〕*adj.* 繁榮的;順遂的

## 13. My Favorite Food

Eggs are my favorite food. I like eggs for several reasons. *Firstly*, eggs are very nutritious: they contain protein which is good for our health. *Secondly*, they always taste good, no matter how they are cooked. *What's more*, cooking and eating them is very easy. *Lastly*, eggs are not expensive, and can be eaten every day.

Eggs often accompany other foods, adding to their fine taste. *For me*, two slices of toast with a fried egg is the best choice for breakfast. Some cooks think adding eggs to soup can make the flavor of the soup better. Small as eggs are, they are an important ingredient of many dishes and so it would be hard to imagine food without eggs.

# 13. 我最喜歡的食物

蛋是我最喜歡的食物。我喜歡蛋的原因有好幾個。首先，蛋十分營養：它含有對健康有益的蛋白質。其次，不管用什麼方式烹調，蛋嚐起來總是十分可口。而且，煮蛋、吃蛋一點也不麻煩。最後一點是，蛋並不貴，每天吃也無妨。

蛋常搭配其他食物，使食物的味道更好。對我而言，兩片吐司夾炒蛋，是早餐的最佳選擇。有些廚師認為，在湯裏加蛋，可使湯的味道更好。蛋雖然小，卻是許多菜餚重要的材料，因此食物中沒有蛋，實在令人很難想像。

**＊＊** ─────────────────────

nutritious〔nju'trɪʃəs〕*adj.* 營養的
contain〔kən'ten〕*v.* 包含
protein〔'protiɪn〕*n.* 蛋白質
***what's more*** 此外
accompany〔ə'kʌmpənɪ〕*v.* 陪伴；伴隨
add〔æd〕*v.* 增加；添加
slice〔slaɪs〕*n.* 片　　toast〔tost〕*n.* 吐司
soup〔sup〕*n.* 湯　　flavor〔'flevɚ〕*n.* 味道
ingredient〔ɪn'gridɪənt〕*n.* 原料

##  14. My Favorite Movie

A few months ago, I had the opportunity to see "The Sound of Music". It is a classic I had always longed to see. The movie is famous for its melodious music, which has remained famous even after such a long time. When the music is combined with the picturesque location scenes, the result is a movie that is really wonderful.

I appreciate this film because it is different from most of today's movies. It contains no violence. *In fact*, it is inspiring and delightful. *It takes us into a dreamy world where we can allow our thoughts to fly free*. It must be because of this that it has remained so popular with both children and adults for so long. And it is also the reason why I will never forget this movie.

## 14. 我最喜歡的電影

幾個月前，我終於有機會欣賞到「眞善美」這部影片。這是一部我一直很想看的經典作品。這部電影以其十分動聽、長久以來仍聲名不墜的音樂而聞名。當音樂配上如畫般的場景，便造就出一部絕佳的影片。

我欣賞這部電影，因爲它和時下大多數的影片不同。這部影片中沒有暴力。事實上，觀賞這部電影還能激勵人心，令人十分愉快。它帶領我們進入一個夢幻般的世界，讓我們的思想自由飛翔。一定是因爲這樣，所以長久以來，它一直受到孩子和大人們的喜愛。這也是我永遠不會忘記這部電影的原因。

\*\*

***The Sound of Music*** 眞善美【電影名】
classic (ˈklæsɪk ) *n.* 經典之作　　long ( lɔŋ ) *v.* 渴望
melodious ( məˈlodɪəs ) *adj.* 旋律優美的
picturesque (ˌpɪktʃəˈrɛsk ) *adj.* 如畫的
***location scene*** 外景
appreciate ( əˈpriʃɪˌet ) *v.* 欣賞
violence (ˈvaɪələns ) *n.* 暴力
inspiring ( ɪnˈspaɪrɪŋ ) *adj.* 激勵的
delightful ( dɪˈlaɪtfəl ) *adj.* 令人愉快的
dreamy (ˈdrimɪ ) *adj.* 夢幻般的
free ( fri ) *adv.* 自由地　　remain ( rɪˈmen ) *v.* 仍然

##  15. My Favorite Musical Instrument

My favorite musical instrument is the piano. I started playing it when I was five. It pleased me to make the sounds by touching the keyboard. *Every day after school, the first thing I would do was play my piano.* I was always soothed by playing it. Soon, with practice, I was able to play beautiful music.

Many people stop playing the piano when they reach a certain level of skill. They never master the instrument. *Fortunately*, because of my mother, this never happened. She always taught me with great patience. *At first*, she tried hard to get me really interested in playing the piano. When I was tired and discouraged, she always encouraged me. *Thanks to her, I have cultivated an everlasting love for the piano.*

## 15. 我最喜歡的樂器

　　我最喜歡的樂器是鋼琴。我從五歲時，就開始彈鋼琴。彈著琴鍵，便能發出聲音，使我很高興。每天放學後，我第一件要做的事，就是彈鋼琴。彈著鋼琴，我的心情就能平靜下來。不斷地練習之後，很快地，我就能彈奏出美妙的音樂。

　　很多人在到達某種程度時，便停止彈琴。他們一直都無法精通這項樂器。我很幸運，因為我的母親，這樣的事從未發生在我身上。她總是很有耐心地教導我。一開始，她非常努力地想讓我對彈鋼琴很有興趣。當我疲倦和氣餒時，她總是鼓勵我。因為她的緣故，使我一直對鋼琴十分地熱愛。

**

instrument〔ˈɪnstrəmənt〕*n.* 器具；樂器
***musical instrument*** 樂器
please〔pliz〕*v.* 取悅；使高興
master〔ˈmæstɚ〕*v.* 精通　　keyboard〔ˈkiˌbord〕*n.* 鍵盤
soothe〔suð〕*v.* 撫慰；使平靜
certain〔ˈsɝtn̩〕*adj.* 某種；某個
level〔ˈlɛvl̩〕*n.* 程度　　skill〔skɪl〕*n.* 技巧
discouraged〔dɪsˈkɝɪdʒd〕*adj.* 氣餒的
encourage〔ɪnˈkɝɪdʒ〕*v.* 鼓勵
***thanks to*** 由於　　cultivate〔ˈkʌltəˌvet〕*v.* 培養
everlasting〔ˌɛvɚˈlæstɪŋ〕*adj.* 永遠的

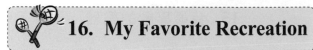

# 16. My Favorite Recreation

I believe that "*All work and no play makes Jack a dull boy*." There have been times in my life when I did nothing but work or study. During such times I felt bored, lonely and depressed.

So I try to get some recreation whenever I can. Playing badminton is the most suitable exercise for me because I can be energetic without being exhausted. Good movies can stimulate the mind. *These activities can help me relax in mind and body*. I think they are essential to my life.

# 16. 我最喜歡的娛樂

　　我認為，「只工作而不遊戲，會使人變得遲鈍。」在我的一生中，曾經有段時間只是在讀書或工作。那時我覺得很無聊、寂寞，而且十分沮喪。

　　所以如果可能的話，我會儘量從事一些娛樂活動。打羽毛球就是最適合我的運動，因為可以使我充滿活力，而且不至於筋疲力盡。而觀賞好的電影可以激勵我的心智。這些活動能幫助我身心都放鬆。我認為在我的生活中，這兩項活動是不可或缺的。

**＊＊** ────────────

recreation〔,rɛkrɪ'eʃən〕*n.* 娛樂；消遣
dull〔dʌl〕*adj.* 遲鈍的
***All work and no play makes Jack a dull boy.***
【諺】只工作而不遊戲，會使人變得遲鈍。
***do nothing but V.*** 一味…；只顧…；光…
depressed〔dɪ'prɛst〕*adj.* 沮喪的
badminton〔'bædmɪntən〕*n.* 羽毛球
suitable〔'sutəbḷ〕*adj.* 適合的
energetic〔,ɛnɚ'dʒɛtɪk〕*adj.* 充滿活力的
exhausted〔ɪg'zɔstɪd〕*adj.* 筋疲力盡的
stimulate〔'stɪmjə,let〕*v.* 激勵
essential〔ə'sɛnʃəl〕*adj.* 必要的；不可或缺的

## 17. My Favorite Season

Flowers blooming, birds chirping, and warm winds blowing—all these are signs that my favorite season, spring, is coming. *Spring drives away the cold of winter and brings forth vigor in all creatures.* The days become longer and the sun rises higher in the sky. There is a joyful energy in the air.

Spring is also the beginning of everything new to me. In spring, I make a brand-new start and make my plans for the coming year. Part of my ritual is a personal "housecleaning." I put away my winter clothes and prepare for warmer weather. It is important to have the feeling of renewing oneself in life. Spring is also an attitude of mind, something to keep even when the seasons change.

## 17.  我最喜歡的季節

　　百花盛開，眾鳥齊鳴，暖風吹拂—這些都是我最喜愛的季節—春天就要到來的景象。春天能趕走冬天的嚴寒，使萬物充滿了活力。白天變得較長，太陽也會高掛在天空。空氣中充滿了快樂的能量。

　　春天對我而言，也是一切新的開始。在春天，我會有個全新的開始，並為未來的一年做好計畫。我迎接春天的部份儀式，就是個人的「大掃除」。我會收起冬衣，為較溫暖的天氣做準備。在生活中，有種全新的感覺是十分重要的。春天也是一種心態，無論季節如何變換，我們仍須保有春天一般的心情。

**\*\*** ——————————————————

　　bloom〔blum〕*v.* 開花
　　chirp〔tʃɝp〕*v.* 啁啾地叫　　sign〔saɪn〕*n.* 跡象
　　*drive away* 趕走　　*bring forth* 產生
　　vigor〔'vɪgɚ〕*n.* 活力　　rise〔raɪz〕*v.* 上升；升起
　　joyful〔'dʒɔɪfəl〕*adj.* 快樂的
　　brand-new〔'brænd'nju〕*adj.* 嶄新的
　　ritual〔'rɪtʃʊəl〕*n.* 儀式
　　housecleaning〔'haʊsˌklinɪŋ〕*n.* 大掃除
　　*put away* 收拾　　renew〔rɪ'nju〕*v.* 更新
　　*attitude of mind* 心態

## 18. My Favorite Song

"Somewhere Out There" is my favorite song. The lyrics are about two people imagining a distant friend beneath the pale moonlight. Although they do not know how far apart they are, they believe that they will meet someday. *I like the poetry of the song, the melodious music, and the singers' voices as well.*

I first heard this song when a friend gave me a CD. She was living abroad, and she gave me the CD as a token of her feelings. *I was moved to tears when I played the song. Nevertheless*, my friend reminded me that soon we would be together again. I then felt reassured. Now I often like to imagine how wonderful it will be when we are together beneath the same bright sky.

## 18. 我最喜歡的歌

"Somewhere Out There"是我最喜歡的一首歌。歌詞是描寫在淡淡的月光下,有兩個人正思念著遠方的朋友。儘管不知道彼此相隔多遠,他們卻相信,總有一天會再相見。我喜歡這首歌所蘊涵的詩意與優美動聽的音樂,以及主唱者的歌聲。

第一次聽見這首歌,是在朋友給我的 CD 裏。她當時住在國外,寄給我這片 CD,代表她的心情。當我播放這首歌時,我不禁感動得落淚。不過,我的朋友提醒我,不久之後我們就會再見面,於是我才覺得比較安心。現在我常喜歡幻想,當我們兩個人一起在同一片明亮的天空下,那會有多棒。

** —————————————————

lyrics〔ˈlɪrɪks〕*n. pl.* 歌詞
imagine〔ɪˈmædʒɪn〕*v.* 想像
beneath〔bɪˈniθ〕*prep.* 在…之下
distant〔ˈdɪstənt〕*adj.* 遙遠的  pale〔pel〕*adj.* 淡淡的
moonlight〔ˈmunˌlaɪt〕*n.* 月光
apart〔əˈpart〕*adv.* 相隔  poetry〔ˈpoɪtrɪ〕*n.* 詩意
melodious〔məˈlodɪəs〕*adj.* 旋律優美的
***as well*** 也(= *too*)  abroad〔əˈbrɔd〕*adv.* 在國外
token〔ˈtokən〕*n.* 象徵  ***be moved to tears*** 感動得落淚
remind〔rɪˈmaɪnd〕*v.* 提醒
reassure〔ˌriəˈʃʊr〕*v.* 使安心

## 19. My Favorite Sport

*Of all the sports, swimming is my favorite. Firstly*, it is beneficial to my health. It can make me stronger and more energetic, and help to keep me slim. *Besides*, it's a good feeling to jump into the cool water on a hot summer day.

Every morning I get up early and swim in the neighborhood pool. During the holidays I like to go to the beach. Swimming in the sea is more fun than swimming in a pool: it is not as crowded, and with all the waves, swimming in it is more challenging and fun.

## 19.  我最喜歡的運動

在所有的運動中,我最喜歡游泳。首先, 游泳有益健康。它能使我更強壯、更有活力, 並幫助我維持苗條的身材。此外,在炎炎夏日 跳進清涼的水中,感覺真棒。

每天早上,我會起得很早,到附近的游泳 池晨泳。假日時,我喜歡去海邊。在海裏游泳 比在游泳池裏游更有趣:那裏比較不擁擠,而 且有許多海浪,在海中游泳更 有挑戰性,也更有樂趣。

\*\*

beneficial〔ˌbɛnəˈfɪʃəl〕*adj.* 有益的

energetic〔ˌɛnəˈdʒɛtɪk〕*adj.* 充滿活力的

slim〔slɪm〕*adj.* 苗條的

neighborhood〔ˈnebəˌhʊd〕*adj.* 附近的

pool〔pul〕*n.* 游泳池(*= swimming pool*)

beach〔bitʃ〕*n.* 海邊

fun〔fʌn〕*adj.* 有趣的　　as〔æz〕*adv.* 一樣地

crowded〔ˈkraʊdɪd〕*adj.* 擁擠的

challenging〔ˈtʃælɪndʒɪŋ〕*adj.* 有挑戰性的

# 20. My Favorite Subject

English has always been my favorite subject. *For me*, becoming interested in English was like being mesmerized; it was something I couldn't resist. I really enjoy reading literature from English-speaking countries. Such books often present interesting ways of looking at the world. I also really like to speak with people from other countries, and knowing English allows me to do this.

English has become the international language. Apart from being a requirement for our exams, it is also essential to many occupations. It is also a language of learning, so *by understanding English, we will have access to the latest information*.

## 20. 我最喜歡的科目

　　英文一直是我最喜歡的科目。對我而言，對英文感興趣，就好像被催眠一般；英文令我難以抗拒。我非常喜歡閱讀英語系國家的文學作品。這些書常會呈現出一種很有趣的世界觀。我也很喜歡和外國人交談，而懂英文使我能夠和他們溝通。

　　英文已經成為國際性的語言。它除了是我們考試必考的科目之外，許多工作都要求必須具備英文能力。此外，英文也是學習者必備的語言，所以學會英文，我們才能獲知最新的資訊。

**　──────────────────────

　　mesmerize〔'mɛsmə,raɪz〕v. 對…催眠；迷惑
　　resist〔rɪ'zɪst〕v. 抵抗；抗拒
　　literature〔'lɪtərətʃɚ〕n. 文學；文學作品
　　present〔prɪ'zɛnt〕v. 呈現
　　allow〔ə'laʊ〕v. 允許；讓
　　***apart from***　除了～之外
　　requirement〔rɪ'kwaɪrmənt〕n. 必要的東西
　　essential〔ə'sɛnʃəl〕adj. 必要的；不可或缺的
　　occupation〔,ɑkjə'peʃən〕n. 職業
　　***have access to***　有接近～的機會
　　latest〔'letɪst〕adj. 最新的

## 21. A Car Accident

On my way back to a family reunion, I witnessed a car accident. It was New Year's Eve, and everyone was eager to get home. At the crossroads, a car ran through a red light and crashed into a gravel truck. The driver was killed instantly and there was a terrible traffic jam.

It was shocking to see the blood everywhere. *For a long time we were stuck in the traffic jam, unable to move.* It was terrible that the driver of the car lost his life. It shows us how important the traffic rules can be. Even if we think we are good drivers, *it is always better to be safe than sorry*.

# 21. 一場車禍

在我要回去和家人團圓的路上，親眼目睹一場車禍。當時是除夕夜，每個人都急著趕回家。就在十字路口，有輛闖紅燈的汽車撞上一部砂石車。司機當場死亡，造成了十分嚴重的交通阻塞。

看到四處都是血，真是令人震驚。有好長一段時間，我們因交通阻塞而動彈不得。看到那位司機死亡真是可怕。這件事告訴我們，交通規則有多重要。即使我們自認為很會開車，但是注意安全總比事後後悔來得好。

\*\* ————————————————

reunion〔ri'junjən〕*n.* 團圓
witness〔'wɪtnɪs〕*v.* 目擊　　***be eager to***　急著要
crossroads〔'krɔs,rodz〕*n. pl.* 十字路口
***run through a red light*** 闖紅燈　　***crash into*** 撞上
gravel〔'grævl̩〕*n.* 碎石　　***gravel truck*** 砂石車
***be killed***　（因意外而）死亡
instantly〔'ɪnstəntlɪ〕*adv.* 立即
terrible〔'tɛrəbl̩〕*adj.* 嚴重的；可怕的
***a traffic jam*** 交通阻塞
shocking〔'ʃɑkɪŋ〕*adj.* 令人震驚的
stuck〔stʌk〕*adj.* 動彈不得的
***It's better to be safe than sorry***. 安全總比後悔好。

## 22. A Diary

May 22

I went to a lecture in the afternoon today. The school invited two Studio Classroom teachers to deliver a lecture on the differences between Chinese and American cultures. I found it a refreshing change to have an English lecture instead of a Chinese one. The lecturers made the speech entertaining, so I learned and enjoyed myself at the same time.

There are many differences between the two cultures, both important and minor. Often small differences such as the Chinese custom of removing shoes before entering a house, or not knowing what to say when meeting someone, cause small embarrassments. If we are more aware of the differences, then we can avoid such difficulties.

# 22. 日記一則

5 月 22 日

　　今天下午我去聽了一場演講。學校邀請兩位「空中英語教室」的老師，來演講關於中美文化之間的差異。由於聽的是英文演講而非中文演講，對我而言，是種令人耳目一新的改變。兩位演講者把演說的內容講解得十分有趣，所以我既可學習，同時又覺得很愉快。

　　中美文化之間有許多大大小小的差異。有些小差異，例如中國人進門之前必須脫鞋的習俗，或是與人見面時不知該說些什麼，都會引起一些有點尷尬的情況。如果我們能多了解其間的差異，就可以避免這樣的問題。

**\*\***————————————

diary〔ˋdaɪərɪ〕*n.* 日記　　lecture〔ˋlɛktʃə〕*n.* 演講
***deliver a lecture*** 發表演說
refreshing〔rɪˋfrɛʃɪŋ〕*adj.* 令人耳目一新的
***instead of*** 而不是　　lecturer〔ˋlɛktʃərə〕*n.* 演講者
entertaining〔͵ɛntəˋtenɪŋ〕*adj.* 有趣的
minor〔ˋmaɪnə〕*adj.* 較不重要的
remove〔rɪˋmuv〕*v.* 除去；脫掉
embarrassment〔ɪmˋbærəsmənt〕*n.* 令人尷尬的事
***be aware of*** 知道；察覺到
difficulty〔ˋdɪfə͵kʌltɪ〕*n.* 困難；問題

## 23. A Fine Night

Once I spent a starry night with friends at in the mountains of Miau-li. I rarely stay up late, but after we had each taken a bath that night, no one felt like sleeping so we went to the park.

*The night was quiet and there were many bright stars*. We all sat on the seesaw, singing songs. Now and then we would stop and enjoy the silence or whisper to one another, and then someone would think of another song and we would sing again. *In this way*, time went by until finally we all felt tired. Although this was a long time ago, I still treasure the memory of that night.

## 23. 美好的夜晚

　　有一次，我和一些好朋友在苗栗的山上，渡過一個星光燦爛的夜晚。我很少熬夜，但是那天晚上，當我們每個人都洗完澡之後，大家都不想睡，所以我們就一起到公園去。

　　那天晚上非常安靜，夜空中佈滿了許多明亮的星星。我們全都坐在蹺蹺板上唱著歌。偶爾我們會停下來，享受四周的寧靜，或是彼此小聲地交談，接著有人想到另一首歌曲，我們就又繼續唱歌。就這樣，時間漸漸過去，直到最後我們大家都覺得疲倦為止。儘管這是好久以前的事了，我仍然十分珍惜那天晚上的回憶。

**　────────────────

starry〔'stɑrɪ〕*adj.* 佈滿星星的
rarely〔'rɛrlɪ〕*adv.* 很少　　***stay up*** 熬夜
***take a bath*** 洗澡　　***feel like V-ing*** 想要～
seesaw〔'si,sɔ〕*n.* 蹺蹺板
***now and then*** 偶爾（= *occasionally*）
silence〔'saɪləns〕*n.* 寂靜
whisper〔'hwɪspɚ〕*v.* 低聲說
***in this way*** 如此一來　　***go by*** （時間）過去
treasure〔'trɛʒɚ〕*v.* 珍惜

# 24. A Horrible Experience

I used to take a shortcut when I was late coming home. One night I had taken the shortcut, and I was walking down a deserted street when I noticed a tall man following me. I walked faster, but he was still here. *In a panic I turned into another street, but found to my horror that it was a dead end.*

I stopped, not daring to look back. "Give me your wallet," said the man. I handed him my wallet, scared to death of what he might do. Suddenly, there was laughter and I turned around to see that the man was my neighbor. He had only been trying to scare me. Although I was lucky that time, now I am afraid to come home late, and I never take shortcuts.

# 24. 一次可怕的經驗

我以前如果很晚回家，都會走捷徑。有天晚上在我走捷徑的時候，走在一條人煙稀少的街道，我注意到有個很高的男人跟著我。我越走越快，還是無法擺脫他。我很驚慌地轉進另一條街，但恐怖的是，那竟是一條死巷。

我停了下來，不敢轉頭去看。那男人說：「皮夾拿出來。」我把皮夾交給他，嚇得要死，不知道他會做些什麼。突然間，他笑了起來，我轉身一看，原來那人是我的鄰居。他只是想嚇唬我而已。儘管那次我很幸運，但現在我很怕太晚回家，而且也不敢再走捷徑了。

**\*\*** ————————————————

horrible〔ˈhɑrəbḷ〕*adj.* 可怕的　　***used to*** 以前
shortcut〔ˈʃɔrtˌkʌt〕*n.* 近路；捷徑
***take a shortcut*** 抄近路；走捷徑
deserted〔dɪˈzɝtɪd〕*adj.* 無人跡的；荒涼的
notice〔ˈnotɪs〕*v.* 注意到　　panic〔ˈpænɪk〕*n.* 恐慌
***in (a) panic*** 驚慌地　　horror〔ˈhɑrɚ〕*n.* 恐怖
***to one's horror*** 令某人感到恐怖的是
***dead end*** 死巷　　dare〔dɛr〕*v.* 敢
***look back*** 回頭看　　hand〔hænd〕*v.* 拿給
scare〔skɛr〕*v.* 使驚嚇
***be scared to death*** 嚇得要死

# 25. A Letter

February 12

Dear Jenny,

I can hardly wait to tell you about my wonderful trip to South Taiwan. It is really the most incredible and interesting trip that I have ever had. Of the things I have seen so far, what impressed me most was the sunrise at Mt. Ali. It was the first time that I ever got up earlier than the sun and watched it rise. You said you enjoyed watching sunsets. Maybe you should pay a visit to Mt. Ali, and then you might prefer sunrises to sunsets.

*Every day is getting tougher and tougher because of the approach of the college entrance exam*. I wonder how you are doing. I have done my best to prepare for the exam, and so am not going to worry any more about the result. After having seen such a spectacular sunrise, I was inspired. *There is always hope for the future*.

Sincerely,
Alice

# 25. 一封信

2 月 12 日

親愛的珍妮：

　　我幾乎等不及要告訴妳，我那次很棒的南台灣之旅。那真的是我最不可思議，而且也是最有趣的一次旅行。在我所見過的事物中，最令我印象深刻的，就是阿里山的日出。這是我第一次起得比太陽早，並看著它升起。妳說妳很喜歡欣賞日落的美景，也許妳該到阿里山一趟，或許妳就會更喜歡日出。

　　由於大學入學考試即將來臨，日子變得一天比一天辛苦。我想知道妳過得好嗎？我已經盡力為這次考試做準備，因此不管結果如何，我都不會再煩惱。在看過如此壯觀的日出後，給了我很大的啟示。未來總是充滿希望的。

愛麗絲　敬上

**

incredible〔ɪnˈkrɛdəbļ〕*adj.* 不可思議的
*so far* 到目前為止　　impress〔ɪmˈprɛs〕*v.* 使印象深刻
Mt.〔maʊnt〕*n.* …山（= *Mount*）
sunrise〔ˈsʌnˌraɪz〕*n.* 日出　　sunset〔ˈsʌnˌsɛt〕*n.* 日落
*pay a visit to* 拜訪　　*prefer* A *to* B 喜歡 A 甚於 B
tough〔tʌf〕*adj.* 困難的　　approach〔əˈprotʃ〕*n.* 接近
do〔du〕*v.* 進展　　spectacular〔spɛkˈtækjələ〕*adj.* 壯觀的
inspire〔ɪnˈspaɪr〕*v.* 激勵

# 26. A Piece of Advice

It is only natural that people are attracted to beautiful things. Being a girl means people often emphasize the importance of your appearance. I was always interested in beauty, so I spent a lot of money on clothes and pretty things. My mother has always told me that *beauty is only skin deep, and that goodness beneath the surface is more important. However*, at first I was too young to take this advice to heart.

But after I started going to senior high school, I realized the true nature of beauty. *A person's value is not something you can calculate from their looks*. There are many things we should learn about a person beneath the surface before we make a judgment. This does not mean that we cannot enjoy physical beauty in ourselves and others, it just means that we should take a more balanced point of view.

# 26. 一項忠告

　　會被美麗的事物所吸引，是很自然的。只要是女孩子，別人就常常會注意妳的外表。我一向對美的事物感興趣，所以花了很多錢，去買衣服以及漂亮的東西。媽媽總是告訴我，美麗是膚淺的，內心的善良更重要。但是我當時還太小，並沒把這項忠告放在心上。

　　但是在我就讀高中之後，我才了解，美的真正本質是什麼。一個人的價值不是從外表就可以衡量的。在我們評斷別人之前，除了外表之外，還有許多事情是我們應該要注意的。這不是說我們不能欣賞別人和自己的外在美，而是應該要抱持著更公平的觀點。

**　＊＊**

advice〔əd'vaɪs〕*n.* 忠告；勸告
emphasize〔'ɛmfə‚saɪz〕*v.* 強調；注重
***Beauty is only skin deep.***【諺】美麗是膚淺的；
　判斷事物不可只看其表面。
goodness〔'gʊdnɪs〕*n.* 善良
beneath〔bɪ'niθ〕*prep.* 在～之下　　surface〔'sɝfɪs〕*n.* 表面
***take*** sth. ***to heart*** 把某事放在心上　　nature〔'netʃɚ〕*n.* 本質
calculate〔'kælkjə‚let〕*v.* 計算；判斷
looks〔lʊks〕*n. pl.* 外表　　physical〔'fɪzɪkl̩〕*adj.* 身體的
***physical beauty*** 外在美
balanced〔'bælənst〕*adj.* 均衡的；公平的
***point of view*** 觀點

# 27. A Quarrel

A terrible quarrel occurred last night. I quarreled with my younger brother, because he refused to do the household chores which by custom we share to help our parents. After dinner, I reminded my brother to wash the dishes, but he ignored me, causing me to shout at him. He shouted back excuses and still refused to do the work. Angered by his indifference, I rushed out of the room.

In retrospect, it is terrible for siblings to quarrel over such trivial matters. As his elder sister, I should have been more tolerant, as getting angry produced nothing except bad feelings. If I had controlled my anger, perhaps the dishes would have been done, and I wouldn't regret being angry now. This quarrel taught me a lesson: before getting angry, one should pause, calm down and think of a solution to the problem.

## 27. 一次吵架的經驗

　　昨天晚上發生了一場很嚴重的爭吵。我和弟弟吵架，因為他拒絕做家事，按照慣例，這些家事應該是我們兩個為了幫忙爸媽，共同分擔的。吃完晚餐後，我提醒弟弟要洗碗，但是他對我不理不睬，使我忍不住對他大聲吼叫。他也以各種藉口對我吼，就是不肯洗碗。他這種不在乎的態度使我很生氣，我就衝出了房間。

　　事後想想，姊弟之間竟會為了這種瑣事爭吵，真是太糟糕了。身為姊姊的我，應該要多容忍他，因為生氣除了傷感情之外，無濟於事。如果我能沈得住氣，也許那些碗早就洗好了，現在我也不會因為生氣而後悔。這次的爭吵給了我一個教訓：生氣之前，最好先停下來冷靜一下，想想問題的解決之道。

**　——————————————————————

　　quarrel〔'kwɑrəl〕*n. v.* 手吵
　　terrible〔'tɛrəbḷ〕*adj.* 可怕的；嚴重的
　　chores〔tʃɔrz〕*n. pl.* 雜事　　***household chores*** 家事
　　custom〔'kʌstəm〕*n.* 慣例　　ignore〔ɪg'nor〕*v.* 忽視；不理會
　　excuse〔ɪk'skjus〕*n.* 藉口　　anger〔'æŋgɚ〕*v.* 激怒　*n.* 怒氣
　　indifference〔ɪn'dɪfərəns〕*n.* 漠不關心
　　rush〔rʌʃ〕*v.* 衝　　retrospect〔'rɛtrə,spɛkt〕*n.* 回想
　　***in retrospect*** 回想；回顧　　siblings〔'sɪblɪŋz〕*n. pl.* 兄弟或姊妹
　　trivial〔'trɪvɪəl〕*adj.* 瑣碎的　　tolerant〔'tɑlərənt〕*adj.* 寬容的
　　***do the dishes*** 洗碗　　lesson〔'lɛsṇ〕*n.* 教訓
　　pause〔pɔz〕*v.* 停下來　　***calm down*** 冷靜下來
　　solution〔sə'luʃən〕*n.* 解決之道 < to >

**28. A Shopping Experience**

My mother and I both like shopping. Last Sunday, we went shopping at the night market. We walked there since it was not far away. By the time we arrived, the street was already crowded with shoppers looking for bargains. Despite the great crowds of people, we felt excited about shopping in such a place.

***We came home loaded with things we had bought***. My father complained that we should not buy things on impulse. Both of us were so happy about our new clothes that we ignored what he said. ***However***, when we tried on the clothes the next day, we found that not all of the clothes fit. We were both upset about it, but there was nothing we could do. We learned a good lesson about buying things.

# 28. 一次逛街的經驗

媽媽和我都很喜歡逛街。上個星期天，我們一起去逛夜市。因為不會很遠，所以我們就走路去。抵達時，街上已經擠滿了逛街的人潮，大家都想買便宜貨。儘管人潮擁擠，在這裏逛街還是令我們覺得很興奮。

回家時，我們帶著買到的東西滿載而歸。爸爸抱怨我們不該因一時的衝動而買東西。我們倆正因為新衣服而高興，所以沒理會他說的話。然而，隔天我們試穿衣服時，才發現不是所有的衣服都很合身。我們兩個都覺得很生氣，但卻無計可施。這次買東西的經驗，給了我們一個很好的教訓。

** ——————————————————

*night market* 夜市

crowd〔kraʊd〕v. 擠滿　n. 人群

*be crowded with* 擠滿了

bargain〔'bɑrgɪn〕n. 便宜貨

load〔lod〕v. 滿載；裝滿

complain〔kəm'plen〕v. 抱怨

impulse〔'ɪmpʌls〕n. 衝動

*on impulse* 一衝動之下　　ignore〔ɪg'nɔr〕v. 忽視

*try on* 試穿　　fit〔fɪt〕v. 適合；合身

upset〔ʌp'sɛt〕adj. 不高興的

lesson〔'lɛsn̩〕n. 教訓

# 29. An Embarrassing Experience

I am not good at recognizing faces, and this
drawback often causes me embarrassment.
*Sometimes* I greet others happily, only to find that
they are not acquaintances of mine. *Other times*
someone pats me on the shoulder and says hello, and
I have no idea who the person is even after saying
good-bye.

*One day* I met a boy on the bus. He started
talking to me like an old friend. While responding
to his conversation, I tried hard to think of his name.
*As usual*, I couldn't think of it even though we had
a pleasant conversation. *However*, when my friends
called my name, he froze. Then he began to apologize
for mistaking me for his friend. He asked me why I
had spoken to him as an old friend. Embarrassed,
I apologized and admitted that, in fact, I hadn't
known who he was even while I was talking to him.
It was a very embarrassing experience.

# 29. 一次尷尬的經驗

　　我不擅長認人，而這項缺點常使我非常尷尬。有時我興高采烈地和人打招呼，結果卻發現我們並不認識。有時別人拍我肩膀和我打招呼，我甚至直到和那人說再見後，還不知道他是誰。

　　有一天，我在公車上遇見一個男孩，他就像老朋友似的開始和我說話。在和他交談的時候，我很努力地想他的姓名。和往常一樣，雖然我們聊得很愉快，我仍然想不起他是誰。然而，當我朋友叫我的名字時，他呆住了。然後他開始道歉，說他把我誤認為是他的朋友。他問我為什麼會像老朋友一樣和他聊天。我尷尬地道歉，並承認其實和他說話時，我並不知道他是誰。這真是一次非常尷尬的經驗。

**

embarrasing〔ɪm'bærəsɪŋ〕*adj.* 令人尷尬的
recognize〔'rɛkəg,naɪz〕*v.* 認得
drawback〔'drɔ,bæk〕*n.* 缺點
***cause sb. sth.*** 給某人帶來某物
greet〔grit〕*v.* 和…打招呼　　***only to V.*** 結果卻…
acquaintance〔ə'kwɛntəns〕*n.* 認識的人
pat〔pæt〕*v.* 輕拍　　***have no idea*** 不知道
respond〔rɪ'spɑnd〕*v.* 回應　　***as usual*** 像往常一樣
freeze〔friz〕*v.* 呆住　　apologize〔ə'pɑlə,dʒaɪz〕*v.* 道歉
***mistake A for B*** 把 A 誤認為 B　　admit〔əd'mɪt〕*v.* 承認

## 30. **An Experience with Dreams**

Dreaming has long been a topic of discussion. *In ancient times*, people depended on dreams to make important decisions, for dreams were regarded as God's will. *Nowadays*, of course, we think of dreams differently. Psychiatrists tell us that they are a common phenomenon which happen to everyone, and that we don't have to guide our lives by them.

I used to have the same dream. I was sitting by the window on a train enjoying the view. Being happy, I began to sing. The other passengers all looked up wondering what was wrong with me, complaining that I had disturbed them. *I was so embarrassed that I wanted to hide*. Suddenly the train went through a dark tunnel. *I was relieved when I awoke to find it was only a dream*.

# 30. 做夢的經驗

　　長久以來，做夢一直是人們討論的話題。在古代，人們會依賴夢來做重要的決定，因爲夢被認爲是上帝的旨意。當然，現在我們對夢的看法已有所不同。精神病醫師告訴我們，做夢是每個人都會有的現象，我們不需要把夢當作是人生的指引。

　　我以前會做同樣的夢。夢見自己坐在火車上，臨窗欣賞風景。因爲很高興，所以我就唱起歌來。其餘的乘客全都抬頭看我，想知道我是怎麼了，還抱怨說我打擾了他們。我尷尬得很想躲起來。突然間，火車穿越一座黑暗的隧道。當我醒來，發現這只是一場夢時，我鬆了一口氣。

**

ancient〔'enʃənt〕*adj.* 古代的
***in ancient times*** 在古代　　***be regarded as*** 被認爲是
will〔wɪl〕*n.*（神的）旨意；天意
psychiatrist〔saɪ'kaɪətrɪst〕*n.* 精神病醫師
common〔'kɑmən〕*adj.* 常見的
phenomenon〔fə'nɑmə,nɑn〕*n.* 現象
guide〔gaɪd〕*v.* 指引　　***used to*** 以前　　view〔vju〕*n.* 景色
***look up*** 抬頭看　　wonder〔'wʌndɚ〕*v.* 想知道
complain〔kəm'plen〕*v.* 抱怨
disturb〔dɪ'stɝb〕*v.* 打擾　　tunnel〔'tʌnḷ〕*n.* 隧道
relieve〔rɪ'liv〕*v.* 使放心；使鬆了一口氣
awake〔ə'wek〕*v.* 醒來

**31. An Unforgettable Trip**

I took the most unforgettable trip in my life last summer. My friends and I traveled by train around the island. We set off at midnight and slept on the train. The train went all the way down to Kaohsiung. By dawn we had arrived at our first stop.

Skipping the popular scenic spots, we decided to visit each of the little towns we passed by. In each case we made efforts to appreciate the local culture and customs. We found it very rewarding. We met many friendly and interesting people and we were shown a lot of hospitality. *It was the most special and informative trip I have ever had.*

# 31. 一次難忘的旅行

　　我一生中最難忘的旅行，就是去年夏天的那一次。我和朋友搭火車環島旅行。我們半夜出發，並且在火車上過夜。火車一路南下開往高雄。清晨時，我們就抵達了第一站。

　　我們決定跳過那些受歡迎的景點，而去探訪我們經過的小城鎮。在每個地方，我們都很努力地欣賞當地的文化和風俗習慣，覺得十分有收穫。我們遇見許多和善而且有趣的人，很熱情地招待我們。這是我所經歷過，最特別，而且也是最能增進知識的旅行。

\*\* ────────────────

unforgettable〔͵ʌnfɚ`gɛtəbḷ〕*adj.* 令人難忘的
***set off*** 出發　　　dawn〔dɔn〕*n.* 黎明；清晨
***first stop*** 第一站　　　skip〔skɪp〕*v.* 略過；跳過
scenic〔`sinɪk〕*adj.* 風景優美的
spot〔spɑt〕*n.* 地點　　case〔kes〕*n.* 情況
appreciate〔ə`priʃɪ͵et〕*v.* 欣賞
local〔`lokḷ〕*adj.* 當地的　　find〔faɪnd〕*v.* 覺得
rewarding〔rɪ`wɔrdɪŋ〕*adj.* 值得做的；有意義的
hospitality〔͵hɑspɪ`tælətɪ〕*n.* 好客；熱情招待
informative〔ɪn`fɔrmətɪv〕*adj.* 增進知識的

## 32. Earthquakes

An earthquake is one of the most terrible natural disasters. In some countries, such as Japan, earthquakes occur frequently due to the country's geographical location. *A major earthquake can kill many people, as well as destroy a lot of property.*

Although it was once thought impossible, scientists are now learning how to predict earthquakes. Knowing when and where an earthquake will occur can save many lives. We in Taiwan should always be prepared. We should make sure our homes and workplaces are earthquake-resistant. We should also demand that all new buildings be safe ones.

# 32. 地　震

　　地震是最可怕的天然災害之一。在某些國家,例如日本,由於國家所處的地理位置,所以經常會發生地震。重大的地震可能會造成許多人死亡,以及財產方面的損失。

　　科學家現在正在學習如何預測地震,這曾經被認為是不可能的。知道地震會發生於何時、何地,可以拯救許多人的生命。在台灣的我們,應該要隨時做好準備。我們要確定居家與工作場所都有防震的設備,而且也應該要求,所有新的建築物都必須是很安全的。

\*\*　————————————————

earthquake〔ˋɝθˌkwek〕*n.* 地震（= *quake*）
disaster〔dɪˋzæstɚ〕*n.* 災難
***natural disaster*** 天災　　***due to*** 由於
geographical〔ˌdʒiəˋgræfɪkl̩〕*adj.* 地理上的
major〔ˋmedʒɚ〕*adj.* 重大的
***as well as*** 以及　　destroy〔dɪˋstrɔɪ〕*v.* 破壞;摧毀
property〔ˋprɑpɚtɪ〕*n.* 財產　　once〔wʌns〕*adv.* 曾經
predict〔prɪˋdɪkt〕*v.* 預測　　***make sure*** 確定
workplace〔ˋwɝkˌples〕*n.* 工作場所
resistant〔rɪˋzɪstənt〕*adj.* 有抵抗力的;耐…的
demand〔dɪˋmænd〕*v.* 要求
***demand that*** + *S.* + (***should***) + *V*原 要求…

## 33. How I Spend Sundays

Sunday is my favorite day of the week because it is my day off. Having a whole day to myself allows me to do what I want. After a pleasant Sunday, I feel refreshed and ready to face the new week.

On Sundays I like to play games with my family. Often we play checkers or badminton, or go for a walk. We especially like to go shopping or go to see a movie. On Sunday evening we kids give our mother a rest and make the dinner ourselves. Unfortunately, our cooking is never as good as hers. ***However***, we enjoy helping our mother and working together. I always have a good time on Sundays.

## 33. 我如何渡過星期天

星期天是我一週內最喜歡的日子，因爲這是我的休假日。擁有屬於自己的一整天，讓我可以做自己想做的事。度過了一個快樂的星期天後，我會覺得精神爲之一振，可以準備面對全新的一週。

在星期天我喜歡和家人同樂。通常我們會下西洋棋或打羽毛球，或是去散步。我們尤其喜歡逛街或是看電影。星期天晚上我們這些小孩會讓媽媽休息，自己做晚餐。遺憾的是，我們的手藝沒有她好。不過我們很喜歡幫媽媽，也很喜歡一起分工合作。星期天我總是過得很愉快。

---

**

off〔ɔf〕*adv.* 休息
to〔tə〕*prep.*【表附屬】…的
allow〔ə'laʊ〕*v.* 允許；讓
pleasant〔'plɛznt〕*adj.* 令人愉快的
refresh〔rɪ'frɛʃ〕*v.* 使恢復精神
checkers〔'tʃɛkəz〕*n. pl.* 西洋棋
badminton〔'bædmɪntən〕*n.* 羽毛球
*go for a walk* 去散步
unfortunately〔ʌn'fɔrtʃənɪtlɪ〕*adv.* 不幸地；遺憾地
*work together* 合作　　*have a good time* 玩得愉快

## 34. How I Spent Yesterday Evening

Yesterday evening was really the worst night I ever had. Unable to concentrate on my studies, I found myself sitting restlessly at my desk staring at my books. My brain went blank for a long time, but when I came to myself, it was even worse. I began to worry about the next day's exam, imagining that I could not pass it. ***The more I thought***, ***the more upset I was. Finally***, I felt like crying.

At ten o'clock, my parents came to comfort me. Mother brought me my favorite apple pie, while Father gave me a beautiful necklace. They comforted me by saying that as long as I had done my best to prepare for the exam, I would have nothing to be ashamed of. Feeling much better, I was finally able to sleep. Now, I am not worrying about the exam results because of the understanding of my parents.

## 34. 我如何渡過昨晚

　　昨天晚上真的是我一生中最難過的一晚。我無法專心讀書，我發現自己不安地坐在書桌前，盯著桌上的書看。有好長一段時間，我的腦中都一片空白，但是當我清醒時，情況變得更糟。我開始擔心隔天的考試，想著自己一定考不上。愈想愈心煩，最後我真想哭。

　　十點的時候，爸媽過來安慰我。媽媽帶來了我最喜歡的蘋果派，而爸爸送給我一條美麗的項鍊。他們安慰我說，只要我盡力準備考試，那麼就不必覺得愧咎。心情好多了之後，我終於睡得著了。現在，由於我爸媽的諒解，我再也不擔心考試的成績了。

**＊＊** —————————————————

unable〔ʌnˋebḷ〕*adj.* 不能⋯的
***concentrate on*** 專心於　　studies〔ˋstʌdɪz〕*n. pl.* 課業
restlessly〔ˋrɛstlɪslɪ〕*adv.* 不安地
***stare at*** 瞪著　　***go blank*** 變成一片空白
***come to*** oneself 清醒　　imagine〔ɪˋmædʒɪn〕*v.* 想像
upset〔ʌpˋsɛt〕*adj.* 不高興的；心煩的
necklace〔ˋnɛklɪs〕*n.* 項鍊
comfort〔ˋkʌmfɚt〕*v.* 安慰　　***as long as*** 只要
***do*** one***'s best*** 盡力　　***be ashamed of*** 因～而覺得羞恥
results〔rɪˋzʌlts〕*n. pl.* 成績

**35. Meeting an Old Friend**

I met an old friend on a bus yesterday. She was my best friend in junior high school, but we had not seen each other since graduation, although I had often thought of her. We used to talk a lot, keeping each other company and studying together. *Since graduation, however, we had gone our separate ways*.

Meeting her was a delight. It was surprising to see how much she had changed in appearance, but as we talked, I found that nothing would ever change our friendship. She still laughed at my tedious jokes, and I was still familiar with her way of talking. *I realize that true friends remain true friends despite a long period of separation*.

# 35. 與老友相逢的經驗

　　昨天我在公車上遇見了一位老朋友。她是我國中時最好的朋友,雖然我時常想起她,但自從畢業以後,我們就沒再見過面了。以前我們經常在一起聊天、讀書。然而,自從畢業之後,我們就各奔前程了。

　　遇見她真令人高興。雖然她外表的改變令人驚訝,但當我們談話時,我發現永遠沒有任何事物能改變我們的友誼。她聽到我沈悶的笑話還是會笑,而我也依舊熟悉她說話的方式。我終於了解,真正的朋友不論分離多久,仍然是真正的朋友。

\*\*

graduation〔͵grædʒʊ'eʃən〕*n.* 畢業

***used to*** 以前　　***a lot*** 常常

***keep sb. company*** 陪伴某人

separate〔'sɛpərɪt〕*adj.* 不同的;各自的

***go our separate ways*** 我們各奔前程

delight〔dɪ'laɪt〕*n.* 高興的事

ever〔'ɛvɚ〕*adv.* 會;在任何時候

tedious〔'tidɪəs〕*adj.* 沈悶的

remain〔rɪ'men〕*v.* 仍然是

despite〔dɪ'spaɪt〕*prep.* 儘管

period〔'pɪrɪəd〕*n.* 期間

# 36. Misunderstandings

A misunderstanding is like an infectious disease. If the symptoms are not treated immediately, the disease will spread. *Not resolving a misunderstanding can gradually spoil the relations between people.*

*Once*, I had a bad misunderstanding with a friend. The friend was an hour late for our meeting. *Finally*, being tired of waiting, I left in a rage. *At the same time, however*, she was waiting angrily at another corner. We had confused the meeting place. *The next day*, we refused to talk to each other. *Eventually*, a mutual friend found out the truth and we made up again. *People should always communicate their true feelings to avoid misunderstandings.*

# 36. 誤　會

誤會就像傳染病一樣，如果有症狀而不立刻治療，這個疾病就會蔓延開來。如果誤會不化解，就可能會逐漸破壞人與人之間的關係。

有一次，我和朋友發生了很嚴重的誤會。約好要見面，她卻遲到了一個小時。最後，我等得很不耐煩，便生氣地走了。然而，就在這個時候，她卻在另一個角落生氣地等候。原來我們弄錯了見面的地點。隔天，我們彼此都不說話。最後，我們一位共同的朋友發現了真相，我們才又和好。人與人之間應該要常表達自己心中真正的感覺，才能避免誤會。

**＊＊** ───────────────

misunderstanding〔ˌmɪsʌndə'stændɪŋ〕 *n.* 誤會
infectious〔ɪn'fɛkʃəs〕 *adj.* 傳染性的
symptom〔'sɪmptəm〕 *n.* 症狀　　treat〔trit〕 *v.* 治療
spread〔sprɛd〕 *v.* 蔓延　　resolve〔rɪ'zɑlv〕 *v.* 解決
gradually〔'grædʒʊəlɪ〕 *adv.* 逐漸地
spoil〔spɔɪl〕 *v.* 破壞　　relation〔rɪ'leʃən〕 *n.* 關係
bad〔bæd〕 *adj.* 嚴重的　***be tired of*** 厭倦
rage〔redʒ〕 *n.* 憤怒　***in a rage*** 在憤怒之中
confuse〔kən'fjuz〕 *v.* 弄錯　　refuse〔rɪ'fjuz〕 *v.* 拒絕
eventually〔ɪ'vɛntʃʊəlɪ〕 *adv.* 最後
mutual〔'mjutʃʊəl〕 *adj.* 共同的
***find out*** 發現；查明　　***make up*** 和好
communicate〔kə'mjunəˌket〕 *v.* 傳達；溝通

##  37. My Experience of Learning English

When I began to learn English in junior high school, it was a terribly difficult subject for me. I could not understand the pronunciation and strange grammar, and because of this, I would fall asleep in class and get bad grades. *One day*, a foreigner asked me for directions. Not understanding what he said, I ran away in embarrassment. *From then on*, I started working hard on my English.

The first step was to pay attention in class and hand my homework in on time. At night I listened to Studio Classroom and ICRT on the radio to improve my listening ability. On the bus I memorized vocabulary. In only one year my English improved greatly. *I believe that where there is a will, there is a way.* You can achieve what you want if you are determined enough.

# 37. 我學英文的經驗

　　當我在國中開始學英文時，我覺得英文是個非常困難的科目。我無法了解英文的發音和奇怪的文法，因此上課時常會睡著，所以成績很差。有一天，有個外國人向我問路。由於聽不懂他說的話，所以我很尷尬地跑掉。從那時起，我就開始努力學英文。

　　我第一個步驟，就是上課時很專心，並準時交作業。晚上我會收聽「空中英語教室」和 ICRT，以增進我的英文聽力。搭公車時，我會背單字。僅僅一年的時間，我的英文已大有進步。我相信「有志者，事竟成」。只要有足夠的決心，就能得到自己想要的。

\*\* ─────────────────────

terribly〔'tɛrəblɪ〕*adv.* 非常地
pronunciation〔prə,nʌnsɪ'eʃən〕*n.* 發音
grammar〔'græmɚ〕*n.* 文法　　***fall asleep*** 睡著
grade〔gred〕*n.* 成績　　foreigner〔'fɔrɪnɚ〕*n.* 外國人
directions〔də'rɛkʃənz〕*n. pl.*（行路的）指引；指示
***ask sb. for directions*** 向某人問路
***pay attention*** 注意；專心　　***hand in*** 繳交
memorize〔'mɛmə,raɪz〕*v.* 背誦；記憶
vocabulary〔və'kæbjə,lɛrɪ〕*n.* 字彙
***Where there is a will, there is a way.***
【諺】有志者，事竟成。
achieve〔ə'tʃiv〕*v.* 達到；（經努力而）獲得
determined〔dɪ't3mɪnd〕*adj.* 堅決的；下定決心的

# 38. On My Way to School

Every morning, I take the bus to Taipei Station, and walk through 228 Peace Park to school.  I always seem to see something interesting along the way.  *Therefore*, I never find it boring, even though I have walked along this route hundreds of times.

*Most of all*, I admire the elderly people gathered in the park.  I enjoy watching them playing badminton, dancing, or walking their pets.  They are always there in good or bad weather, and seem content to watch the busy world go by.  When I look at their tranquil and contented faces, I feel inspired.

# 38. 上學途中

　　每天早上，我都搭公車到台北車站，並走過二二八和平公園到學校。在上學途中，我似乎總能看見一些有趣的事。因此，即使這條路我已經走了好幾百次，還是不覺得無聊。

　　我特別欽佩那些聚集在公園裏的老人。我喜歡看他們打羽毛球、跳舞，或帶寵物散步。無論天氣是好是壞，他們總是在那裏，而且似乎很滿足地觀看來往忙碌的世界。看著他們寧靜與滿足的臉，給了我很大的啟示。

**

find〔faɪnd〕v. 覺得　　route〔rut〕n. 路線
***most of all*** 特別；尤其　　admire〔əd'mɪr〕v. 欽佩
elderly〔'ɛldəlɪ〕adj. 老的
badminton〔'bædmɪntən〕n. 羽毛球
walk〔wɔk〕v. 帶（寵物）散步；遛
pet〔pɛt〕n. 寵物
content〔kən'tɛnt〕adj. 滿足的；滿意的（= *contented*）
tranquil〔'træŋkwɪl〕adj. 寧靜的
inspired〔ɪn'spaɪrd〕adj. 得到啟發的

**39. Rainy Days**

Rainy days are annoying for most people. Such days are inconvenient because you have to carry an umbrella with you. And your clothes and shoes will get covered in mud. On rainy days it is easier to catch cold, and it is guaranteed that the traffic on a rainy day will always be worse than that on a sunny day.

*However*, I like rainy days. In summer, walking in a drizzling rain can be romantic as well as cool. Watching a rainstorm from inside is also quite fine, especially when there is thunder and lightning. It is very nice to be safe in bed with lightning flashing outside.

# 39. 下雨天

　　對大部分的人來說，下雨天是最令人心煩的。下雨天很不方便，因為必須隨身攜帶雨傘。衣服與鞋子也會沾上泥巴。下雨天比較容易感冒，而且交通情況一定會比晴天時來得糟。

　　不過，我還是喜歡下雨天。夏日裏，走在濛濛細雨中，既浪漫又涼爽。在室內看暴風雨也相當不錯，尤其是有打雷閃電的時候。能在床上安穩地看著屋外的閃電，真的很棒。

**\*\***————————————————————

annoying〔ə'nɔɪɪŋ〕*adj.* 令人心煩的
cover〔'kʌvɚ〕*v.* 覆蓋；蓋滿 < *in* ; *with* >
mud〔mʌd〕*n.* 泥巴　　***catch cold*** 感冒
guarantee〔ˌgærən'ti〕*v.* 保證
sunny〔'sʌnɪ〕*adj.* 晴朗的
drizzling〔'drɪzḷɪŋ〕*adj.* 細雨濛濛的
romantic〔ro'mæntɪk〕*adj.* 浪漫的
***as well as*** 以及　　rainstorm〔'renˌstɔrm〕*n.* 暴風雨
inside〔ɪn'saɪd〕*n.* 裡面；內部
thunder〔'θʌndɚ〕*n.* 雷
lightning〔'laɪtnɪŋ〕*n.* 閃電
flash〔flæʃ〕*v.* 閃爍；閃過

## 40. The Most Satisfying Thing I Have Ever Done

The most satisfying thing I have ever done is to work as a volunteer for a charity. I believe I have benefited a lot from this experience. I have made lots of new friends and learned how they deal with difficulties. *I also have realized that giving is more satisfying than taking*. Giving some of my time to others has made me more mature and considerate.

My favorite task is to read for the blind on Sundays. With the responsibility of preparing materials on my own, I am like a teacher. When I am going to read to young children, I always try to choose something interesting, like a fairy tale, to stimulate their imagination. When reading, I try to use different voices for the characters to make the story more exciting. I think that after three years of practice, I have become good at telling stories, and there is always satisfaction in doing something well.

# **40. 我最滿意的事**

　　我所做過最滿意的事，就是去慈善機構擔任義工。我相信我從這項經驗獲益良多。我結交了許多新朋友，並學習他們處理困難的方法。我也體認到施比受更令人滿足。撥出自己的一些時間給別人，使我變得更成熟、更體貼。

　　我最喜歡的工作，就是在週日唸書給盲人聽。因爲我必須自己負責準備題材，所以就像個老師一樣。當我要唸書給年幼的孩子聽時，我一定會設法選擇有趣的內容，例如童話故事，來激發他們的想像力。在閱讀時，我會試著用不同的聲音，來代表不同的人物，使故事更刺激。經過三年的練習之後，我想我已經變得很會說故事，能把某件事做好，總是會令人覺得很滿足。

\*\* ────────────────

***work as*** 擔任　　volunteer〔͵vɑlən'tɪr〕*n.* 志願者；義工
charity〔'tʃærətɪ〕*n.* 慈善機構　　benefit〔'bɛnəfɪt〕*v.* 獲益
***make friends*** 交朋友　　***deal with*** 應付；處理
mature〔mə'tʃʊr〕*adj.* 成熟的
considerate〔kən'sɪdərɪt〕*adj.* 體貼的（= *thoughtful*）
task〔tæsk〕*n.* 任務；工作　　***the blind*** 盲人
***on*** one's ***own*** 自己　　***fairy tale*** 童話故事
stimulate〔'stɪmjə͵let〕*v.* 刺激
character〔'kærɪktɚ〕*n.* 人物　　***be good at*** 擅長

## 41. Typhoons

Typhoons usually strike Taiwan between July and September, doing a lot of damage to the island. The heavy rains which come with the typhoons often result in floods, which can affect farms and lead to price increases for vegetables. The winds, too, can be dangerous, as they can destroy houses and property.

To reduce damage, you need to take some precautions. *Firstly*, you should listen to the weather reports to keep informed about approaching typhoons. When a typhoon is coming, you should store food and water and make sure windows and doors are secure. *In case of a blackout*, *you should prepare flashlights or candles*. Preparations such as these can lessen worries about typhoons.

# 41. 颱 風

颱風通常在每年的七月到九月之間侵襲台灣，造成很大的損害。伴隨颱風而來的豪雨，常導致水災，影響農田，並使蔬菜的價格上揚。強風也可能十分危險，會摧毀房舍與財產。

為了減少颱風所造成的損害，我們必須採取一些預防措施。首先，應該收聽氣象報告，以熟知颱風的動向。當颱風來臨時，應該要儲存食物和水，並確定門窗是否安全無虞。為了以防萬一停電，應該先準備手電筒或蠟燭。這些預防措施能夠減輕我們對於颱風的憂慮。

\*\* ────────────────

strike〔straɪk〕v. 侵襲　　***do damage to***　損害

***heavy rain***　大雨　　***result in***　導致；造成

flood〔flʌd〕n. 水災　　increase〔'ɪnkris〕n. 增加

destroy〔dɪ'strɔɪ〕v. 破壞；損毀

property〔'prɑpɚtɪ〕n. 財產

precaution〔prɪ'kɔʃən〕n. 預防措施

informed〔ɪn'fɔrmd〕adj. 消息靈通的

approaching〔ə'protʃɪŋ〕adj. 即將來臨的

store〔stor〕v. 儲存　　secure〔sɪ'kjur〕adj. 安全的

***in case of***　以防萬一　　blackout〔'blæk,aut〕n. 停電

flashlight〔'flæʃ,laɪt〕n. 手電筒

candle〔'kændḷ〕n. 蠟燭　　lessen〔'lɛsn̩〕v. 減少

## 42. When I Feel Lonely

Many people today claim not to feel lonely because they always have so many things to do. *For some*, there is never enough time to make money. *For others*, there are so many appointments, dates with friends and social occasions that there just isn't time to feel lonely or bored. *For students*, being bored or feeling lonely can make them feel guilty. They know they could be studying. With all these things to occupy us, having spare time can seem out of the ordinary, and that can be what we regard as loneliness.

The best way to avoid loneliness is to cultivate a hobby. *For me*, playing the violin is the best way to relieve loneliness. Music is very effective as it has a mood of its own. It changes our mood when we listen to it. It also brings me satisfaction as it is something I have learned through my own hard work. With just a little effort and imagination, the feeling of loneliness can disappear.

# 42. 當我感到寂寞時

　　現在有很多人都說，他們不會感到寂寞，因為總是有許多事要做。對有些人來說，賺錢的時間永遠都不夠。有些人則是和朋友的約會、交際應酬太多，根本沒有時間感到寂寞或無聊。對學生而言，無聊或寂寞可能會讓他們有罪惡感，因為他們知道可以把這些時間用來讀書。有這些事讓我們忙，若有多餘的時間，似乎是很不尋常的，也許這就是我們所認為的寂寞。

　　避免寂寞最好的方法，就是培養嗜好。對我而言，拉小提琴是排解寂寞最好的方法。音樂對於消除寂寞很有效，因為音樂本身就包含某種心情。當我們聽音樂時，心情會隨之而改變。音樂也能帶給我滿足感，因為它是我努力學習的成果。只要有一點努力與想像力，寂寞的感覺就能消失。

**

lonely〔'lonlı〕*adj.* 寂寞的　　claim〔klem〕*v.* 宣稱
social〔'soʃəl〕*adj.* 社交的　　occasion〔ə'keʒən〕*n.* 場合
guilty〔'gɪltɪ〕*adj.* 有罪惡感的
occupy〔'ɑkjəˌpaɪ〕*v.* 使忙碌　　***spare time*** 空閒時間
***out of the ordinary*** 異常的　　regard〔rɪ'gɑrd〕*v.* 認為
loneliness〔'lonlɪnɪs〕*n.* 孤獨；寂寞
cultivate〔'kʌltəˌvet〕*v.* 培養
violin〔ˌvaɪə'lɪn〕*n.* 小提琴　　relieve〔rɪ'liv〕*v.* 減輕
effective〔ə'fɛktɪv〕*adj.* 有效的　　mood〔mud〕*n.* 心情

# 43. A Grateful Heart

On the streets of Taipei, I often spot some poor men begging for money. Usually they are crowded into a corner, wearing ragged clothes. Sometimes in the winter, they seem frozen by the cold. When I see this, I cannot help feeling sympathy for them, and I realize how lucky I am.

*We should be grateful for and satisfied with all the things we are provided with*. There are many people in the world dying of hunger. The next time we begin to mutter our dissatisfaction, we should think of those dispossessed and disheartened people. Maybe then we will appreciate our blessings.

# 43. 常懷感謝心

　　在台北街頭，我常看到一些可憐人在乞討錢。通常他們會擠在角落裏，穿著十分破爛的衣服。有時在冬天，他們似乎會因爲天冷而被凍僵了。當我看到這種現象，我就忍不住對他們十分同情，也才了解到自己有多幸運。

　　對於別人提供給我們的一切，我們應該心存感激，並感到滿足。在這世界上，有許多人死於饑餓。下次當我們因爲不滿而開始抱怨時，應該想一想那些無依無靠、十分沮喪的人。也許那樣，我們就會對自己所擁有的幸福心存感激。

**

grateful〔'gretfəl〕adj. 感激的　　spot〔spɑt〕v. 看到
beg〔bɛg〕v. 乞討　　*be crowded into* 擠進
ragged〔'rægɪd〕adj. 破爛的　　freeze〔friz〕v. 使結冰
*cannot help* + *V-ing* 忍不住～
sympathy〔'sɪmpəθɪ〕n. 同情
provide〔prə'vaɪd〕v. 提供；供應
*die of hunger* 餓死　　mutter〔'mʌtɚ〕v. 抱怨
dispossessed〔,dɪspə'zɛst〕adj. 無依無靠的
disheartened〔dɪs'hɑrtṇd〕adj. 沮喪的
then〔ðɛn〕adv. 那時；若是那樣
appreciate〔ə'priʃɪˌet〕v. 感激；欣賞
blessing〔'blɛsɪŋ〕n. 幸福

#  44. A House Is Not a Home

"House" and "home" are two words that have a similar meaning, which often confuses people. "House" and "home" both refer to places which people live in. ***However***, there is a slight difference between them. "Home" is often referred to as the place that we live in with our families. Sadly, in our society, people can hardly distinguish a home from a house because they often see no difference between them. This confusion can be traced back to the indifference between family members. ***Therefore***, we can tell that love is an important factor in a home.

A home is a shelter, not only for our bodies but also for our minds. Whenever we are depressed, we can go home for comfort. Everyone in the family will do their best to take care of each other and share their happiness as well as sorrow. Without love, a home is merely a house where loneliness is all that can be found. ***In conclusion***, a house can never be a home unless there is love.

# 44. 房子不能算是家

「房子」和「家」這兩個字意思十分相似，常使人覺得困惑。「房子」和「家」都是指人們居住的地方，然而，兩者之間卻有一些細微的差異。「家」通常是指我們和家人一起居住的地方。遺憾的是，在我們的社會中，人們不太能分辨「家」和「房子」，因爲常常覺得二者並沒有什麼不同。這種混淆不清的現象，其原因可追溯到家庭成員之間，彼此漠不關心所致。因此，我們可以知道，愛是「家」十分重要的因素。

家是我們身體與心靈的避風港。每當我們心情沮喪時，可以回家尋求安慰。家裏的每個成員會盡力互相照顧，並彼此分享快樂與分擔悲傷。如果沒有愛，那麼「家」便只是一個充滿寂寞的「房子」。總之，除非有愛，不然「房子」就永遠不能算是個「家」。

** ————————————————

confuse〔kən'fjuz〕*v.* 使混淆　　***refer to*** 是指
slight〔slaɪt〕*adj.* 些微的　　***be referred to as*** 被稱爲
sadly〔'sædlɪ〕*adv.* 可悲的是；遺憾的是
distinguish〔dɪs'tɪŋgwɪʃ〕*v.* 分辨
***can be traced back to*** 可追溯到
indifference〔ɪn'dɪfərəns〕*n.* 漠不關心
tell〔tɛl〕*v.* 知道　　factor〔'fæktɚ〕*n.* 因素
shelter〔'ʃɛltɚ〕*n.* 避難所　　***not only…but also*** 不僅…而且
depressed〔dɪ'prɛst〕*adj.* 沮喪的　　comfort〔'kʌmfɚt〕*n.* 安慰
***as well as*** 以及　　sorrow〔'saro〕*n.* 悲傷
merely〔'mɪrlɪ〕*adv.* 僅僅；只　　***in conclusion*** 總之

# 45. Buying Books

While other girls like to go shopping for beautiful clothes, I like to shop for books. *After all*, *clothes can only decorate our appearances*, *while books can beautify our minds*. Wherever there are good books, you'll find me there.

Most of my books are novels, essays, poems and biographies. *In addition*, I also like comic books. Serious literature can help broaden my intellectual horizons and develop my thinking skills, whereas comic books can entertain me when I am bored and in no mood for serious works. Books are appropriate for all occasions.

# 45. 買　書

　　雖然其他女孩子喜歡逛街買漂亮的衣服，我卻喜歡買書。畢竟，衣服只能裝飾我們的外表，而書卻能美化我們的心靈。凡是有好書的地方，就可以在那裏找到我。

　　我的書大部份是小說、散文、詩集，與名人傳記。此外，我也喜歡漫畫書。嚴肅的文學作品能幫助我拓展知識領域，並培養我的思考技巧，然而當我覺得無聊，沒心情看一些嚴肅的作品時，漫畫書能讓我覺得很愉快。所以書在任何時候都適用。

**\*\***

*shop for* 購買　　*after all* 畢竟

decorate〔ˈdɛkəˌret〕*v.* 裝飾

while〔hwaɪl〕*conj.* 然而（= *whereas*）

beautify〔ˈbjutəˌfaɪ〕*v.* 美化　　essay〔ˈɛse〕*n.* 散文

poem〔ˈpo‧ɪm〕*n.* 詩

biography〔baɪˈɑgrəfɪ〕*n.* 傳記　　*comic book* 漫畫書

literature〔ˈlɪtərətʃɚ〕*n.* 文學；文學作品

broaden〔ˈbrɔdṇ〕*v.* 拓展

horizons〔həˈraɪznz〕*n. pl.* 知識範圍；眼界

develop〔dɪˈvɛləp〕*v.* 培養

entertain〔ˌɛntɚˈten〕*v.* 娛樂；使快樂

mood〔mud〕*n.* 心情　　work〔wɝk〕*n.* 作品

appropriate〔əˈproprɪɪt〕*adj.* 適當的；合適的

occasion〔əˈkeʒən〕*n.* 時候；場合

## 46. City Life and Country Life

*In my opinion*, there are many reasons for preferring country life to city life. *For one thing*, country people are more easygoing. City people are usually in a rush, but people in the countryside can take their time doing things. Environmental conditions in the country are also better than those in the city. The countryside is cleaner, quieter, and prettier.

*However*, living in the city also has its advantages. *For example*, jobs are more easily available and more varied. City residents also have better access to public facilities such as libraries, museums, concerts, and other cultural events, and are more in touch with the pulse of this rapidly changing world.

# 46. 都市生活與鄉村生活

　　我認為,喜歡鄉村生活甚於都市生活的原因有很多。首先,鄉村居民的生活比較悠哉。都市裡的人總是很匆忙,但是住在鄉下的人,做事比較從容不迫。鄉下的生活環境也比都市的好。鄉下比較乾淨、安靜,而且比較美麗。

　　然而,住在都市裏也有優點。舉例來說,在都市裏工作較容易找,而且種類也比較多。都市居民能很方便地利用公共設施,像是圖書館、博物館、音樂會、或其他文化活動,而且也比較能掌握這個快速變遷的世界的脈動。

\*\* ─────────────

country〔ˈkʌntrɪ〕adj. 鄉下的　n. 鄉下
**prefer A to B** 喜歡 A 甚於 B　　**for one thing** 首先
easygoing〔ˈizɪˈgoɪŋ〕adj. 悠哉的　　**in a rush** 匆忙
countryside〔ˈkʌntrɪˌsaɪd〕n. 鄉村地區
**take** one's **time** 不慌不忙;慢慢來
conditions〔kənˈdɪʃənz〕n. pl. 狀況;情況
available〔əˈveləbḷ〕adj. 可獲得的
varied〔ˈvɛrɪd〕adj. 各種的;不同的
resident〔ˈrɛzədənt〕n. 居民
access〔ˈæksɛs〕n. 接近或使用的權利
facilities〔fəˈsɪlətɪz〕n. pl. 設施
event〔ɪˈvɛnt〕n. 大型活動
**be in touch with** 完全了解;持續關注
pulse〔pʌls〕n. 脈搏;動向
rapidly〔ˈræpɪdlɪ〕adv. 快速地

# 47. Dealing with Stress

*Living in such a fast-paced society, no one can be free from stress.* A husband may be pushed to earn more money to support his family. A wife may also have to work outside the home as well as do the housework. People everywhere suffer from some kind of stress, and I am no exception. *As a student, I am under great pressure from all the schoolwork and exams.*

Whenever I am under stress, I like to go for a walk and sing songs. Stress can be reduced by a leisurely stroll in a park or along the street. Singing a song can cheer me up when the pressure and worries are making me feel bad. Singing is such a simple thing, but it really helps me. Knowing how to deal with stress is essential for living a good life.

# 47. 如何應付壓力

　　生活在步調如此快速的社會裏，沒人能免於壓力。丈夫可能爲了要負擔家計，被迫去賺更多的錢。妻子也可能必須出外工作以及做家事。所有的人都承受著某種壓力，而我也不例外。身爲學生，我承受著來自學校課業和考試的沈重壓力。

　　每當我有壓力時，我喜歡去散散步、唱唱歌。在公園或街道上悠閒地散步，可以減輕壓力。當壓力和煩惱使我心情不好時，唱歌可以讓我振作起來。唱歌是一件很簡單的事，卻對我有很大的幫助。要擁有良好的生活，懂得如何應付壓力是十分必要的。

**

***deal with*** 應付；處理　　stress〔strɛs〕 *n.* 壓力
fast-paced *adj.* 步調快的　　***be free from*** 免於
push〔puʃ〕 *v.* 逼迫　　support〔sə'port〕 *v.* 供養
***as well as*** 以及　　housework〔'haʊs,wɝk〕 *n.* 家事
***suffer from*** 遭受；因…而受苦　　some〔sʌm〕 *adj.* 某一
pressure〔'prɛʃɚ〕 *n.* 壓力
schoolwork〔'skul,wɝk〕 *n.* 功課；學業
***go for a walk*** 去散步　　leisurely〔'liʒɚlɪ〕 *adj.* 悠閒的
stroll〔strol〕 *n.* 漫步；散步
***cheer*** *sb.* ***up*** 使某人振作精神
essential〔ə'sɛnʃəl〕 *adj.* 必要的；不可或缺的

 **48. Eating in Taiwan**

The wide variety of Taiwanese food is world-famous and continues to astonish visitors to the island. All you have to do is go to "Snake Alley" and you will be surprised by the incredible things being eaten there. In Taiwan, you never have to worry about where to eat — inexpensive restaurants are everywhere.

*However*, not everything is safe to eat. You should be careful when eating food bought from street stalls, as it may not be hygienic and may cause stomachaches or worse. *In addition*, one should avoid restaurants which offer the meat of rare or endangered species. But problems seldom occur. *In general*, eating in Taiwan is a wonderful experience.

# 48. 吃在台灣

台灣的食物種類繁多，舉世聞名，一直都讓來台灣的遊客覺得十分驚訝。你只要到萬華的「蛇巷」看一看，就會對那些不可思議的食物吃驚不已。在台灣，你永遠都不需要擔心找不到地方吃東西——便宜的餐廳到處都有。

然而，並非每種食物都是可以安心食用的。如果吃從路邊攤買來的食物，務必要小心，因為不夠衛生的食物可能會使你胃痛，或導致更嚴重的疾病。此外，凡是有供應稀有或瀕臨絕種動物肉類的餐廳，都應該避免。但是這一類的問題並不常發生。一般說來，在台灣吃東西是一個非常棒的經驗。

**＊＊**

variety〔vəˋraɪətɪ〕*n.* 種類；多樣性
world-famous　*adj.* 世界聞名的
astonish〔əˋstɑnɪʃ〕*v.* 使驚訝
***all* one *has to do is* + *V.*** 某人所需要做的就是…
snake〔snek〕*n.* 蛇　　alley〔ˋælɪ〕*n.* 巷子
incredible〔ɪnˋkrɛdəbl̩〕*adj.* 不可思議的
stall〔stɔl〕*n.* 攤販
hygienic〔ˌhaɪdʒɪˋɛnɪk〕*adj.* 衛生的
stomachache〔ˋstʌmək͵ek〕*n.* 胃痛
avoid〔əˋvɔɪd〕*v.* 避開　　rare〔rɛr〕*adj.* 稀有的；罕見的
endangered〔ɪnˋdendʒɚd〕*adj.* 瀕臨絕種的
species〔ˋspiʃɪz〕*n.* 物種【單複數同形】
***endangered species*** 瀕臨絕種的動物
***in general*** 一般說來

# 49. How I Feel About KTV

KTV is very popular in Taiwan, especially with city residents. Under the pressure of city life, many people love to sing in a KTV because they can relax and release their tension. With the low lighting and loud music, people easily forget their shyness and frustrations.

My friends and I often go to a KTV after our monthly exams. The afternoon following the exam we'll spend time singing instead of studying. In the KTV we sing our favorite songs, which keeps us in a good mood. By singing, we also forget about our exams and get a brand-new start for the coming days. *In my opinion, a KTV is a good entertainment place where we can relax and enjoy ourselves*.

# 49. 我對 KTV 的看法

　　KTV 在台灣十分流行，尤其受到都市居民的歡迎。由於都市生活的壓力，很多人很喜歡去 KTV 唱歌，因為這樣可以使自己放鬆，並消除緊張。在微弱的燈光下，聽著大聲的音樂，人們很容易就能忘記害羞與挫折。

　　我和朋友常在月考後去 KTV。考完試的下午，我們會停止讀書，到 KTV 去唱歌。在 KTV 唱著我們最喜歡的歌曲，大家心情都十分愉快。唱歌也能使我們忘記考試，對於往後的日子，有了全新的開始。我認為 KTV 是個很好的娛樂場所，在那裏我們可以放鬆，而且玩得很愉快。

**─────────────────

resident〔ˋrɛzədənt〕 n. 居民　　pressure〔ˋprɛʃɚ〕 n. 壓力
relax〔rıˋlæks〕 v. 放鬆　　release〔rıˋlis〕 v. 釋放
*release one's tension* 消除緊張
low〔lo〕 adj. （設備）開得弱的
lighting〔ˋlaıtıŋ〕 n. 照明；照明設備
shyness〔ˋʃaınıs〕 n. 害羞
frustration〔͵frʌsˋtreʃən〕 n. 挫折　　*monthly exam* 月考
following〔ˋfaloıŋ〕 prep. 在…之後
*instead of* 而不是　　mood〔mud〕 n. 心情
brand-new〔ˋbrændˋnju〕 adj. 全新的
coming〔ˋkʌmıŋ〕 adj. 即將來臨的
entertainment〔͵ɛntɚˋtenmənt〕 n. 娛樂
*enjoy oneself* 玩得愉快

# 50. How I Feel About Night Schools

Night schools play an important role in our educational system. They allow people to continue studying who otherwise would not have the opportunity. For those who cannot go to school in the daytime, night schools are their best choice if they are interested in pursuing higher education.

One drawback is that night school students spend less time at school. *Therefore*, they have fewer opportunities to enjoy a rich school life. *Moreover*, they are often too busy working to participate in extracurricular activities. *However*, most night school students feel that it is worth the sacrifice, and I agree with them.

# 50. 我對夜校的看法

夜校在我們的教育體制中，扮演了重要的角色。它們讓那些原本沒機會讀書的人，可以繼續讀書。對於那些白天無法上學的人而言，如果有興趣接受更高等的教育，夜校就是他們最好的選擇。

夜校的缺點之一，就是讀夜校的學生，在校的時間較少。因此，他們比較沒有機會享受豐富的學校生活。此外，夜校生通常工作太忙碌，無法參與課外活動。然而，大多數的夜校生都覺得，這種犧牲還是值得的，而我也同意他們的看法。

**

allow〔ə'laʊ〕*v.* 讓
otherwise〔'ʌðɚ,waɪz〕*adv.* 不那樣；否則；要不然
daytime〔'de,taɪm〕*n.* 白天　　pursue〔pɚ'su〕*v.* 追求
drawback〔'drɔ,bæk〕*n.* 缺點
rich〔rɪtʃ〕*adj.* 豐富的　　***too…to~*** 太…而不能~
***be busy (in) + V-ing*** 忙於…
participate〔pɚ'tɪsə,pet〕*v.* 參與 < *in* >
extracurricular〔,ɛkstrəkə'rɪkjələ〕*adj.* 課外的
worth〔wɝθ〕*adj.* 值得…的
sacrifice〔'sækrə,faɪs〕*n.* 犧牲

# 51. How I Feel About Taxis

Taxis are often praised for their convenience and comfort. People can take a taxi to go quickly to where they want instead of standing in a slow, jam-packed bus. Taxi drivers usually know the city well and know exactly where your destination is. Despite these advantages, one big drawback is the price. Taking a taxi has become a luxury.

I don't often take taxis, unless I really need to. When I am about to be late for school, or an appointment, taking a taxi can often get me there just in time. *In this way*, I generally don't miss anything important. *Expensive as it is, taking a taxi is sometimes necessary in modern city life*.

## 51. 我對計程車的看法

計程車因為方便又舒適，所以常受到稱讚。人們可以搭計程車迅速抵達想去的地方，不必在又慢又擠的公車上站著。計程車司機通常對市區很熟，能確切地知道你的目的地在哪裏。計程車雖然有這些優點，但卻有個很大的缺點，那就是它的價格。搭計程車已成為奢侈的享受。

除非必要，我不常搭計程車。當我上學或赴約快要遲到時，搭計程車常能讓我及時趕到。這樣一來，我幾乎不曾錯過任何重要的事。雖然搭計程車很昂貴，但在現代的都市生活中，有時是必要的。

**\*\***

*instead of* 而不是
jam-packed〔'dʒæm'pækt〕*adj.* 擠滿的
exactly〔ɪg'zæktlɪ〕*adv.* 確切地
destination〔,dɛstə'neʃən〕*n.* 目的地
advantage〔əd'væntɪdʒ〕*n.* 優點
drawback〔'drɔ,bæk〕*n.* 缺點
luxury〔'lʌkʃərɪ〕*n.* 奢侈（品）
*be about to V.* 即將；快要
*in time* 及時    *in this way* 如此一來
generally〔'dʒɛnərəlɪ〕*adv.* 通常
miss〔mɪs〕*v.* 錯過
*Expensive as it is, …* 雖然它很貴，…
    （= *Though it is expensive, …*）

## 52. I Have a Dream

We cannot live without dreams. Dreams can beautify our tedious lives and give us encouragement to go on. I have a dream that one day I shall travel all over the world with my family.

Father always tells us that traveling is the best way to broaden our minds. And so I have promised myself to do what I can to travel in the future. Having a dream and being committed to it is the way to make it more likely to happen. *Persevere and stick to your dreams, and with a little luck, they will come true.*

# 52. 我的夢想

我們不能沒有夢想。夢想可以美化我們沈悶的生活，鼓勵我們繼續前進。我的夢想是希望有一天，能和家人一起環遊世界。

父親總是告訴我們，旅遊是拓展心智最好的方式。所以我向自己承諾，以後我要盡可能把握旅遊的機會。擁有夢想，並努力去追求，夢想就更有可能實現。不屈不撓地堅持夢想，再加上一點點的運氣，夢想一定會實現。

\*\*

*cannot live without*　不能沒有

beautify〔'bjutə,faɪ〕*v.* 美化

tedious〔'tidɪəs〕*adj.* 沈悶的

*go on*　繼續前進

broaden〔'brɔdn̩〕*v.* 拓展

*be committed to*　致力於

persevere〔,pɝsə'vɪr〕*v.* 堅忍；不屈不撓

*stick to*　堅持

*come true*　實現

## 53. If I Had Only 24 Hours to Live

If I had only 24 hours to live, I would have two important things to accomplish. The first thing would be to express my gratitude and appreciation to those I love. Coming from a traditional Chinese family, I feel inhibited from hugging my mother and telling her how much I love her. ***But if I had only 24 hours to live, I would forget my inhibitions, and give her a big hug***.

The second thing would be to see my family and friends for the last time. I would be reminded of their kindness so that I would never forget them even in the hereafter. I would pray to continue our relationships. After doing these two things, I would feel relaxed about my last 24 hours.

# 53. 如果我只剩二十四小時

如果我只剩二十四小時可活，我有兩件重要的事情想完成。第一件就是要向那些我所愛的人表達感謝。因為我出生於傳統的中國家庭，所以會有所顧忌，不敢擁抱母親，告訴她我有多愛她。但是如果我只剩二十四小時，我會不顧一切，熱情地擁抱她。

第二件事，就是去看我摯愛的家人和朋友最後一次。我會想著他們種種的好處，這樣即使在來生，我也絕不會忘記他們。我會祈禱，希望我們之間的關係可以持續。如果能完成這兩件事，我就可以放心地渡過我最後的二十四小時。

**\*\***────────────────

accomplish〔əˋkɑmplɪʃ〕*v.* 完成
gratitude〔ˋgrætəˏtjud〕*n.* 感激
appreciation〔əˏpriʃɪˋeʃən〕*n.* 感激
traditional〔trəˋdɪʃənḷ〕*adj.* 傳統的
inhibited〔ɪnˋhɪbɪtɪd〕*adj.* 有顧忌的
hug〔hʌg〕*v. , n.* 擁抱
inhibition〔ˏɪnhɪˋbɪʃən〕*n.* 顧忌
***for the last time*** 最後一次　　***be reminded of*** 想起
kindness〔ˋkaɪndnɪs〕*n.* 親切；仁慈
hereafter〔hɪrˋæftɚ〕*n.* 來生
pray〔pre〕*v.* 祈禱　　relaxed〔rɪˋlækst〕*adj.* 輕鬆的

## 54. If I Were a Freshman

If I were a freshman, I would do some of the things I couldn't do in high school. ***For example***, because of preparing for the college entrance exam, I was unable to continue playing the flute. In order to have a good time in college, life has to be balanced between studies and other activities.

I would also like to work part-time, since I never had a chance in high school. I think a little work experience would help me in the future. Employers always like to see that people have worked before. Having a job would also reduce the financial burden on my parents a little.

# 54. 假如我是大學新鮮人

假如我是大學新鮮人，我要做一些高中時不能做的事。譬如說，為了準備大學入學考試，所以我無法繼續吹笛子。想要有愉快的大學生活，學業和其他活動都必須兼顧。

我也想去打工，因為高中時，我從來沒有機會工讀。我認為有一些工作經驗，對我以後會有幫助。老闆總是喜歡有工作經驗的人。有份兼差的工作，也能減輕一點我父母的經濟負擔。

\*\*

freshman〔'frɛʃmən〕*n.* 大一新生
flute〔flut〕*n.* 笛子
balance〔'bæləns〕*v.* 使平衡
studies〔'stʌdɪz〕*n. pl.* 學業
part-time〔'pɑrt'taɪm〕*adv.* 兼差地
employer〔ɪm'plɔɪɚ〕*n.* 僱主；老闆
financial〔faɪ'nænʃəl〕*adj.* 財務上的
burden〔'bɝdn̩〕*n.* 負擔

## 55. If I Were a Billionaire

If I were a billionaire, I would first buy a big house in Tien Mu. The mansion would come with a swimming pool and large yard. In such an environment it would be easier to feel calm and peaceful. After a long vacation, things might get a little boring, so I would begin some activities such as pottery, painting, playing the piano, etc. There are so many things I would like to do.

I know that being rich isn't everything. A rich person has to decide if his friends like him or his money. So I wouldn't want to be very rich. But if something can improve the quality of your life and allow you to be free from working at some boring job, why not take the opportunity?

# 55. 假如我是億萬富翁

　　假如我是億萬富翁，我首先要在天母買棟大房子。這間豪宅會有游泳池和大庭院。在這樣的環境裏，比較能心平氣和。在渡完漫長的假期後，生活可能會變得有點無聊，所以我會開始從事一些活動，如陶藝、繪畫、彈鋼琴等等。我想做的事情非常多。

　　我知道有錢並非一切。有錢人必須判斷朋友喜歡的是他的人，還是他的錢。所以我並不想太富有。但是如果錢財能改善生活品質，使我們不必做一些無聊的工作，這樣的機會為什麼不把握呢？

\*\* ────────────────────

billionaire〔ˌbɪljənˈɛr〕*n.* 億萬富翁
mansion〔ˈmænʃən〕*n.* 豪宅　　　***come with*** 附有
yard〔jɑrd〕*n.* 院子
calm〔kɑm〕*adj.* 平靜的
peaceful〔ˈpisfəl〕*adj.* 平靜的；寧靜的
pottery〔ˈpɑtərɪ〕*n.* 陶器；陶器製造
etc.〔ɛtˈsɛtrə〕…等等
improve〔ɪmˈpruv〕*v.* 改善
allow〔əˈlaʊ〕*v.* 讓　　　***be free from*** 擺脫
some〔sʌm〕*adj.* 某個

**56. Libraries**

Libraries can play an important role in our lives. *First of all*, they can provide us with a great variety of knowledge. We can get most information we need in a good library. *In addition*, libraries can help us if we need help finding a job, finding an address, or if we want to find out how to do something, or where to go on a vacation. We can do all these things and more in a library.

Libraries are also good places to study. *Unfortunately*, I often don't have enough time to read any books other than course textbooks. I hope to make better use of libraries after I pass the college entrance exam.

# 56. 圖書館

　　圖書館在我們的生活中扮演重要的角色。首先，它能提供我們很多各式各樣的知識。在很好的圖書館裏，我們所需要的大部份資料都可以找得到。此外，當我們需要找工作、查住址、尋找做某件事的方法，或是查渡假的地點時，圖書館都可幫得上忙。這些事以及其他的問題，我們都可以在圖書館裏解決。

　　圖書館也是個讀書的好地方。遺憾的是，除了學校的教科書以外，我通常沒有足夠的時間來閱讀其他書籍。希望通過大學入學考試之後，我能更善加利用圖書館。

**\*\*** ────────────────

　　variety〔vəˈraɪətɪ〕*n.* 種類；多樣性
　　*a great variety of* 很多各式各樣的
　　*in addition* 此外
　　address〔əˈdrɛs〕*n.* 住址
　　*find out* 查明　　*go on a vacation* 去渡假
　　*other than* 除了…之外
　　course〔kors〕*n.* 課程
　　textbook〔ˈtɛkstˌbʊk〕*n.* 教科書
　　*make better use of* 更善加利用
　　*entrance exam* 入學考試

# 57. Money

It is hard to overemphasize the importance of money in modern society. Money allows us to meet our basic needs by buying food and clothes. We need to earn enough money to become financially independent so that we don't have to lead a poor life.

*However, there are many things money cannot buy, such as love, health and lost time*. Owning millions in property cannot guarantee happiness. *Therefore*, we should not be slaves to money. We should save it and spend it wisely. Saving and spending our money wisely can help us to realize our dreams.

# 57. 錢

　　在現代社會中，錢的重要性再怎麼強調也不爲過。有錢我們才能購買食物和衣服，滿足基本的需求。我們必須賺足夠的錢，才能在財務方面獨立自主，不致於過著貧困的生活。

　　然而，有許多東西是金錢買不到的，像是愛、健康，以及失去的時間。擁有數百萬的財產，不能保證一定能快樂。因此，我們不該成爲金錢的奴隸。我們應該把錢存起來，並很明智地使用。如果能存錢並明智地使用錢，就可以幫助我們實現夢想。

**

overemphasize〔͵ovɚ'ɛmfə͵saɪz〕*v.* 過份強調
meet〔mit〕*v.* 滿足（需要）
financially〔faɪ'nænʃəlɪ〕*adv.* 財務上
independent〔͵ɪndɪ'pɛndənt〕*adj.* 獨立的
*so that* 以便於　　*lead a ~ life* 過~的生活
lost〔lɔst〕*adj.* 失去的
property〔'prɑpɚtɪ〕*n.* 財產
guarantee〔͵gærən'ti〕*v.* 保證
slave〔slev〕*n.* 奴隸
realize〔'riə͵laɪz〕*v.* 實現

# 58. Music and I

Music plays an important role in my daily life. I like to listen to music when I study and wait for the bus. *Music keeps me company and stops me from getting bored*. At night, just before I go to sleep, music is there, taking away my worries.

Besides listening to music, I also like playing it. I can play the piano and the harmonica. *I find that music helps to lift my spirits when I'm down*. It also gives me a sense of accomplishment when the practice pays off. There are not many things which can help me through the day as much as music.

# 58. 音樂與我

　　音樂在我的日常生活中，扮演很重要的角色。我喜歡在讀書和等公車時聽音樂。音樂能陪伴我，讓我不會覺得無聊。晚上在我入睡之前，總是會有音樂，帶走我所有的煩惱。

　　除了聽音樂之外，我也喜歡彈奏樂器。我會彈鋼琴及吹口琴。我發現當我心情低落時，音樂有助於提振我的精神。練習有了成果時，會使我覺得很有成就感。沒有多少事物能像音樂一樣，幫助我渡過每一天。

**　————————————————

daily〔'delɪ〕*adj.* 每天的；日常的
***daily life*** 日常生活　　***keep sb. company*** 陪伴某人
***stop sb. from V-ing*** 使某人不～
bored〔bord〕*adj.* 覺得無聊的
harmonica〔har'manɪkə〕*n.* 口琴
lift〔lɪft〕*v.* 提高；鼓舞
***lift one's spirits*** 提振某人的精神
down〔daʊn〕*adj.* 沮喪的；情緒低落的
accomplishment〔ə'kamplɪʃmənt〕*n.* 成就
***a sense of accomplishment*** 成就感
***pay off*** 得到回報；成功
through〔θru〕*prep.* 經過；完畢；…終了爲止

# 59. Nearsightedness

Why have more and more young students become nearsighted in recent years? *Some things* have always been bad for the eyes. Studying for the endless exams is one thing all of us have to go through, and often we cannot avoid straining our eyes. But *other things* we can control, such as television and video games. What should we do to avoid eye problems?

We should always try to read in a well-lit room. If we use a computer we should always remember to give our eyes frequent rests. Eating a lot of carrots will also help to preserve good vision. It is actually not difficult to develop good habits for our eyes. As with any activity to do with health, looking after our eyes should be a priority.

# 59. 近 視

　　最近幾年，為什麼有愈來愈多年輕的學生罹患近視？有些事情的確會對眼睛有害。像是我們每個人都必須經歷的，為了應付無止盡的考試，我們常常必須耗費眼力讀書。但還有一些是我們可以控制的，例如看電視和打電動玩具。我們應該怎麼做，才能避免眼睛方面的疾病？

　　我們應該要在照明設備良好的房間閱讀。如果使用電腦，一定要記得讓眼睛經常休息。多吃胡蘿蔔也有助於維護良好的視力。培養良好的視力保健習慣其實並不難。在所有的保健活動中，視力保健應該最優先。

**

nearsightedness〔ˏnɪrˈsaɪtɪdnɪs〕*n.* 近視
nearsighted〔ˈnɪrˈsaɪtɪd〕*adj.* 近視的
recent〔ˈrisn̩t〕*adj.* 最近的
strain〔stren〕*v.* 過度使用而損傷
***video game*** 電動玩具
problem〔ˈprɑbləm〕*n.* 疾病
well-lit〔ˈwɛlˈlɪt〕*adj.* 照明良好的
carrot〔ˈkærət〕*n.* 胡蘿蔔
preserve〔prɪˈzɜv〕*v.* 維護
vision〔ˈvɪʒən〕*n.* 視力　develop〔dɪˈvɛləp〕*v.* 培養
***do with*** 和～有關　***look after*** 照顧
priority〔praɪˈɔrətɪ〕*n.* 優先考慮的事

# 60. Neighbors

It is important to have a good relationship with our neighbors. Neighbors can help to protect our homes. They can also be helpful in an emergency. If you have young children, they can help to keep an eye on them if you are not there. *In general*, our neighborhood will be a happy place if everyone has a spirit of cooperation.

In modern society, people have tended to ignore their neighbors. *However*, in the past, people lived in large communities, like one large family. Socializing with our neighbors is part of being human. It gives us a warm feeling inside and inspires us to do good things.

# 60. 鄰 居

　　和鄰居培養良好的關係是十分重要的。鄰居能幫忙保護我們的家。有緊急情況時，他們也能幫得上忙。我們不在的時候，鄰居也可以幫忙看顧年幼的小孩。一般說來，如果每個人都有互助合作的精神，我們的居家附近，就會是個令人十分愉快的地方。

　　在現代的社會，人們很容易忽略鄰居。然而，在過去，人們居住的大社區，就好像是一個大家庭。和鄰居互相來往，會使我們更有人情味。這樣會使我們的內心覺得十分溫暖，並能激勵我們行善。

**＊＊**

neighbor〔'nebɚ〕*n.* 鄰居
emergency〔ɪ'mɝdʒənsɪ〕*n.* 緊急情況
***keep an eye on*** 看顧　　***in general*** 一般說來
neighborhood〔'nebɚˌhʊd〕*n.* 鄰近地區
cooperation〔koˌɑpə'reʃən〕*n.* 合作
***tend to*** 易於；傾向於
ignore〔ɪg'nor〕*v.* 忽視
community〔kə'mjunətɪ〕*n.* 社區
socialize〔'soʃəˌlaɪz〕*v.* 交際；來往
inspire〔ɪn'spaɪr〕*v.* 激勵

# 61. Newspapers

Newspapers play an important role in modern life. As a kind of mass communication media, the most important function of newspapers is to provide us with various kinds of information. We can know what is going on in our own nation and around the world by reading newspapers.

I am in the habit of reading newspapers every day. *Newspapers help me to keep abreast of the changing world*. Without newspapers, I would feel isolated from the world. Sometimes I read more than two newspapers if I have free time, because I can know more detailed information from different points of view. *Therefore*, I cannot imagine living without newspapers.

# 61. 報　紙

　　報紙在現代生活中，扮演一個很重要的角色。由於報紙是一種大眾傳播媒體，所以它最重要的功能，就是提供給我們各式各樣的資訊。閱讀報紙能讓我們知道國內外所發生的事。

　　我有每天看報紙的習慣。報紙能讓我跟上這個多變的世界。沒有報紙，會使我覺得自己與世界隔絕。如果有空的話，有時我會閱讀兩份以上的報紙，因為我可以從不同的觀點，得知更詳盡的消息。因此，沒有報紙的生活，真是令人無法想像。

**\*\***————————————————

*mass communication*　大眾傳播
media〔'midɪə〕*n. pl.*　媒體
various〔'vɛrɪəs〕*adj.*　各式各樣的
*go on*　發生
*be in the habit of*　有～的習慣
*keep abreast of*　不落後；跟上最新情況
isolated〔'aɪsḷ,etɪd〕*adj.*　隔離的
*free time*　空閒時間
detailed〔'diteld〕*adj.*　詳細的
*point of view*　觀點
imagine〔ɪ'mædʒɪn〕*v.*　想像

## 62. No Pain, No Gain

*"No pain, no gain" reminds us that every success requires effort.* It suggests that if you want to achieve a goal, you cannot do it through idleness, or expect success to come to you easily. Sometimes getting what we want takes determination.

Studying English is an example of this proverb. How can we learn a language so different from our own? We must overcome our embarrassment at making mistakes as well as work hard to master the complex grammar and vocabulary. All these take a long time, but if we persevere, the effort will definitely seem worth it. *The pain of our efforts will turn into the gain of knowing a new language.*

# 62. 一分耕耘，一分收穫

「一分耕耘，一分收穫」，這句名言提醒我們，想要成功，都必須努力。這句話告訴我們，如果想達成目標，就不能懶散，或是期望成功能輕易到手。有時候，必須要有決心，才能得到我們想要的。

學英文就是這句諺語最好的例證。我們要如何才能學好跟自己母語如此不同的語言呢？我們必須克服犯錯時的困窘，並且要努力精通複雜的文法和字彙。這些都需要很長的時間，但如果我們能堅持到底，這些努力一定是十分值得的。我們努力時的辛勞，終將變成收穫，使我們學會一種新的語言。

**\*\***───────────────

***No pain, no gain.*** 【諺】不勞則無獲；一分耕耘，
  一分收穫。美國人通常用 No pain, no gain. 英國人
  常用 No pains, no gains.

remind〔rɪ'maɪnd〕*v.* 提醒；使想起

require〔rɪ'kwaɪr〕*v.* 需要

suggest〔sə'dʒɛst〕*v.* 暗示；顯示

achieve〔ə'tʃiv〕*v.* 達成  idleness〔'aɪdḷnɪs〕*n.* 懶惰

determination〔dɪ,tɜmə'neʃən〕*n.* 決心

overcome〔,ovə'kʌm〕*v.* 克服  ***as well as*** 以及

master〔'mæstə〕*v.* 精通

complex〔'kɑmplɛks〕*adj.* 複雜的

grammar〔'græmə〕*n.* 文法

vocabulary〔və'kæbjə,lɛrɪ〕*n.* 字彙

persevere〔,pɜsə'vɪr〕*v.* 堅忍；不屈不撓

definitely〔'dɛfənɪtlɪ〕*adv.* 一定  ***turn into*** 變成

# 63. On Knowledge

There is a saying that "Knowledge is power." Knowledge can be used to make ourselves and society better. Knowledge can allow us to lead rich lives without great financial wealth. *Knowledge can enlighten us and eliminate foolish superstitions and prejudices*. Knowledge also leads to a lot of inventions which can make our lives easier and more comfortable.

Knowledge is a direct result of a good education and understanding of our experiences. If we have knowledge, we can live our lives confidently even when we are faced with difficulties. We need to keep our minds open and question things in order to make our future better than today.

# 63. 論知識

俗話說：「知識就是力量。」運用知識可以讓我們自己及社會變得更好。就算沒有許多財富，知識也可以讓我們過著很充實的生活。知識可以啓迪我們的思想，消除愚昧的迷信與偏見。知識也帶給我們許多發明，使我們的生活更安逸、更舒適。

知識是良好教育與了解自身經驗的直接成果。如果我們有知識，即使面對困難，也能過得很有自信。我們需要敞開心靈，對事情抱持懷疑的態度，以使我們擁有比今天更美好的未來。

**\*\***─────────────────────

saying〔'seɪŋ〕*n.* 諺語     rich〔rɪtʃ〕*adj.* 豐富的
financial〔faɪ'nænʃəl〕*adj.* 財務上的
wealth〔wɛlθ〕*n.* 財富
enlighten〔ɪn'laɪtn̩〕*v.* 啓迪；啓蒙
eliminate〔ɪ'lɪmə,net〕*v.* 消除
superstition〔,supɚ'stɪʃən〕*n.* 迷信
prejudice〔'prɛdʒədɪs〕*n.* 偏見
***lead to*** 導致；造成
easy〔'izɪ〕*adj.* 舒適的；安逸的
result〔rɪ'zʌlt〕*n.* 成果
confidently〔'kɑnfədəntlɪ〕*adv.* 有自信地
***be faced with*** 面對     question〔'kwɛstʃən〕*v.* 質疑

# 64. On Punctuality

Punctuality is an important virtue, but these days it is often neglected. There is always the excuse of the terrible traffic conditions in Taiwan to explain why we are late, but is this really a good excuse? We should take into account the traffic before we leave, and if necessary, leave a little earlier. There isn't really any excuse for being late.

***Being punctual shows that we are reliable and serious about what we are doing.*** If we are not punctual, we will waste other people's time and create a lot of bad feelings. In order to be punctual, we must organize our time well. Then society will function efficiently and harmoniously.

# 64. 論守時

　　守時是一項重要的美德，然而最近卻常常被人忽略。我們總會以台灣糟糕的交通狀況作爲遲到的藉口，但這眞是個好藉口嗎？在我們動身之前本來就應該先考量交通狀況，如果有需要，就早一點出發。遲到實在是不應該有任何藉口。

　　守時就表示我們是個可信賴的人，並且對正在做的事情很認眞。假如我們不守時，就會浪費別人的時間，使他們不高興。爲了守時，我們必須妥善安排自己的時間，如此一來，我們的社會才能更有效率、更和諧。

**

punctuality〔ˌpʌŋktʃʊˈælətɪ〕*n.* 守時
virtue〔ˈvɝtʃʊ〕*n.* 美德　　***these days*** 最近
neglect〔nɪˈglɛkt〕*v.* 忽略
excuse〔ɪkˈskjus〕*n.* 藉口
***take into account*** 考慮
punctual〔ˈpʌŋktʃʊəl〕*adj.* 守時的
reliable〔rɪˈlaɪəbl̩〕*adj.* 可靠的
organize〔ˈɔrgənˌaɪz〕*v.* 安排
function〔ˈfʌŋkʃən〕*v.* 運作
efficiently〔əˈfɪʃəntlɪ〕*adv.* 有效率地
harmoniously〔harˈmonɪəslɪ〕*adv.* 和諧地

**65. Problems in Summer**

*In summer*, many problems arise because of the hot weather. *In hot weather*, food quickly spoils, which can cause health problems. *At this time*, pests, such as flies and cockroaches, reproduce in great numbers. They pose a health hazard by spreading germs they pick up from garbage. Further problems that occur include power failures and water rationing.

*There are things we can do to prevent these problems*. *First*, we must ensure that food is well-preserved, so we don't eat spoilt food. We should keep our surroundings clean, so as not to encourage flies and roaches. And we should be economical when using electricity and water. If we can stick to these simple guidelines, summer will be more enjoyable.

# 65. 夏天帶來的問題

在夏天，由於天氣炎熱，所以會有許多問題產生。炎熱的天氣使得食物很快就變壞，因而導致健康方面的問題。在這時候，像蒼蠅、蟑螂這類的害蟲，會大量繁殖。牠們會散播從垃圾而來的病菌，危害人體的健康。其他問題還包括停電及限水。

要防止這些問題，有下列幾種方法。首先，我們必須確保食物保存良好，才不會吃到腐敗的食物。我們應該要保持環境整潔，才不會助長蒼蠅與蟑螂滋生。此外，我們應節約用電和用水。如果能遵守這些簡單的原則，我們就能渡過一個更愉快的夏天。

** ─────────────────────────

arise〔ə'raɪz〕v. 發生　　spoil〔spɔɪl〕v. 變壞；腐敗
pest〔pɛst〕n. 害蟲　　fly〔flaɪ〕n. 蒼蠅
cockroach〔'kɑk,rotʃ〕n. 蟑螂 ( = *roach* )
reproduce〔,riprə'djus〕v. 繁殖
*in great numbers* 大量地　　pose〔poz〕v. 引起
hazard〔'hæzəd〕n. 危害　　germ〔dʒɝm〕n. 病菌
*pick up* 獲得　　further〔'fɝðɚ〕adj. 更進一步的
*power failure* 停電　　ration〔'reʃən〕v. 配給
ensure〔ɪn'ʃur〕v. 確保　　preserve〔prɪ'zɝv〕v. 保存
*so as not to V.* 以免～　　encourage〔ɪn'kɝɪdʒ〕v. 助長
economical〔,ikə'nɑmɪkl̩〕adj. 節省的　　*stick to* 遵守
guidelines〔'gaɪd,laɪnz〕n. pl. 指導方針；準則
enjoyable〔ɪn'dʒɔɪəbl̩〕adj. 令人愉快的

##  66. Rising Early

"*The early bird catches the worm*" suggests that we can profit from getting up early in the morning. It is a shame to always lie around in bed and waste the day. There are so many activities, and so little time to do them. *What's more*, breakfast is considered by many doctors to be the most important meal of the day. There's nothing better than a nice, big breakfast.

The weekend is another story. If you don't have any activity to attend, sleeping late is truly one of the great pleasures of life. There you are — perhaps the birds are singing outside, and you are warm and drowsy in bed. Suddenly sleep comes again, and you are sleeping without a care in the world. Rising early is a good thing most of the time, but we can enjoy sleeping, too.

# 66. 早 起

「早起的鳥兒有蟲吃」，這句諺語告訴我們，早上早起有許多好處。老是躺在床上浪費光陰，是件可惜的事。可以從事的活動有很多，但可以利用的時間卻很少。而且，許多醫生認為，早餐是一天當中最重要的一餐。沒有什麼比得上一頓好吃又豐盛的早餐。

週末則是不同的情況。如果沒有什麼活動要參加，晚起的確是人生一大樂事。你就這樣——也許還可聽到有鳥兒在外面唱歌，而你躺在床上，覺得十分溫暖、昏昏欲睡。突然間睡意再度來臨，你可以無憂無慮地沈沈睡去。通常早起是一件好事，但我們還是可以享受睡覺的樂趣。

**\*\***

rise〔raɪz〕*v.* 起床    worm〔wɜm〕*n.* 蟲
*The early bird catches the worm.* 【諺】早起的鳥兒
    有蟲吃；捷足先登。
suggest〔səgˋdʒɛst〕*v.* 顯示；指出
profit〔ˋprɑfɪt〕*v.* 獲益    shame〔ʃem〕*n.* 可惜的事
*lie around* 閒散；悠閒    *what's more* 此外；而且
meal〔mil〕*n.* 一餐    big〔bɪg〕*adj.* 豐盛的
*another story* 另一回事；不同的情形
attend〔əˋtɛnd〕*v.* 參加    *sleep late* 睡過頭
*there you are* 你就這樣
drowsy〔ˋdraʊzɪ〕*adj.* 昏昏欲睡的
care〔kɛr〕*n.* 憂慮的事

# 67. Say "No" to Drugs

Drug abuse has become a serious problem among teenagers these days. Most of them begin to take drugs out of curiosity. *However*, once they start taking drugs, they find it hard to quit and may become addicted. They spend a lot of money buying drugs. If they use up their own money, they often turn to criminal activities, which causes problems for society.

The most important way to stop drug-taking lies in the teenagers themselves. They should try to make good friends and cultivate decent interests. *Besides this*, the government should enact stricter laws to punish drug dealers. *As long as everyone spares no effort to say "No" to drugs, there will be a better and healthier future for society*.

# 67. 向毒品説「不」

　　最近在青少年之間，濫用毒品已成爲十分嚴重的問題。許多青少年都是出於好奇，而開始吸食毒品。然而，一旦他們開始吸毒，就可能會上癮，覺得很難戒除。他們會花很多錢買毒品，如果錢用完了，常常會轉而從事犯罪活動，製造許多社會問題。

　　要阻止吸食毒品，最重要的方式，就在於青少年本身。青少年應該試著結交一些益友，並培養良好的興趣。此外，政府應制定更嚴格的法律，來懲罰販賣毒品的人。只要每個人都能不遺餘力地向毒品說「不」，我們的社會就會有一個更美好、更健康的未來。

**　━━━━━━━━━━━━━━━━━

drug〔drʌg〕*n.* 藥物；毒品　　abuse〔ə'bjus〕*n.* 濫用
***drug abuse*** 濫用毒品　　***these days*** 最近
***take drugs*** 吸毒　　curiosity〔͵kjʊrɪ'ɑsətɪ〕*n.* 好奇
find〔faɪnd〕*v.* 覺得　　quit〔kwɪt〕*v.* 戒除
addicted〔ə'dɪktɪd〕*adj.* 上癮的
***use up*** 用完　　***turn to*** （在遭遇困境時）開始做
criminal〔'krɪmənḷ〕*adj.* 犯罪的
***lie in*** 在於　　cultivate〔'kʌltə͵vet〕*v.* 培養
decent〔'disn̩t〕*adj.* 高尚的；合宜的
enact〔ɪn'ækt〕*v.* 制定（法律）
strict〔strɪkt〕*adj.* 嚴格的　　dealer〔'dilɚ〕*n.* 販賣者
***as long as*** 只要　　***spare no effort*** 不遺餘力

# 68. The Advantages of Bicycle Riding

Bicycle riding has many advantages. Bicycles are as economical as buses, but you don't have to wait for them. They are as convenient as cars, able to go anywhere at any time, and *what's more*, can easily avoid traffic jams. And their advantage over cars and buses is that they are pollution-free, so they do not harm the environment.

Riding a bicycle is also very good exercise. Nowadays most people don't get enough exercise, especially in the city where many people sit at desks all day. *Bicycles can be an important part of a healthy life style.*

# 68. 騎腳踏車的好處

　　騎腳踏車有許多好處。騎腳踏車和搭公車一樣省錢，而且又不必等。腳踏車也和汽車一樣方便，隨時都可以去任何地方，而且也比較能避免塞車。腳踏車比汽車或公車好，是因為腳踏車無污染，所以不會破壞環境。

　　騎腳踏車也是一種很好的運動。現在大部份的人運動量都不夠，特別是都市裡有很多人整天都坐在辦公桌前。腳踏車可算是健康生活中十分重要的一部份。

\*\* ──────────────

　　economical〔ˌikəˋnɑmɪkl̩〕adj. 節省的
　　**what's more** 此外　　jam〔dʒæn〕n. 阻塞
　　**a traffic jam** 交通阻塞（= *traffic congestion*）
　　free〔fri〕adj. 沒有…的
　　pollution-free adj. 無污染的
　　harm〔hɑrm〕v. 損害
　　nowadays〔ˋnɑʊəˌdez〕adv. 現在
　　healthy〔ˋhɛlθɪ〕adj. 健康的；有益健康的
　　**life style** 生活方式

# 69. The Career I Want to Devote Myself to

*I have long thought being a doctor would be the ideal career for me*. In my family, everyone has something to do with medicine, and this, no doubt, influenced my decision to become a doctor. I have a natural interest in biology and medicine, so it makes sense that I want to be a doctor. I have studied hard to qualify for medical school.

I realize that interest alone is not enough to be a doctor. I must also have dedication and maturity. Although being a doctor is a heavy responsibility, I think overcoming a challenge can make life more rewarding.

# 69. 我想從事的職業

　　長久以來，我一直認為當醫生是我最理想的職業。我的家人從事的都是與醫藥方面有關的工作，所以無疑地，這也是影響我決定要當醫生的因素。我本來就對生物學和醫學很有興趣，所以想當醫生是理所當然的事。為了有資格進醫學院，我很努力用功。

　　我知道當醫生光有興趣是不夠的。我也必須要有犧牲奉獻的熱忱，以及成熟的人格。儘管醫生的責任重大，但我認為，能克服挑戰，人生才更有意義。

**　——————————————————

career〔kəˋrɪr〕*n.* 職業；一生的事業
***devote oneself to*** 致力於　　ideal〔aɪˋdiəl〕*adj.* 理想的
***have something to do with*** 和～有關
***no doubt*** 無疑地　　influence〔ˋɪnfluəns〕*v.* 影響
natural〔ˋnætʃərəl〕*adj.* 自然的；天生的
***make sense*** 有意義；合理
qualify〔ˋkwɑləˏfaɪ〕*v.* 有資格　　***medical school*** 醫學院
alone〔əˋlon〕*adv.* 單單；僅僅
dedication〔ˏdɛdəˋkeʃən〕*n.* 獻身；熱忱
maturity〔məˋtʃurətɪ〕*n.* 成熟
overcome〔ˏovɚˋkʌm〕*v.* 克服
challenge〔ˋtʃælɪndʒ〕*n.* 挑戰
rewarding〔rɪˋwɔrdɪŋ〕*adj.* 有意義的；值得的

# 70. The Harm Caused by Smoking

Smoking, as everybody knows, is hazardous to your health. It can cause cancer in smokers as well as in passive smokers. According to statistics, a large number of people die every year of cancer and other diseases related to smoking. *Not only* is this a great loss for their families, *but* society *also* spends a lot of money to pay for their health care.

*Up to now*, smoking has been regarded as an acceptable pastime. *In fact*, nicotine is a drug, and smokers become addicted to it. With so much evidence to show how bad smoking is, the next time someone asks: "Do you mind if I smoke?", we should say, "Yes, I mind for you, and for me."

# 70. 抽煙的害處

　　大家都知道，抽煙會危害健康。不僅抽煙的人，連吸入二手煙的人，都會因而罹患癌症。根據統計，每年都有許多人死於與抽煙有關的癌症或其他的疾病。這不但是他們家庭的重大損失，社會也會花很多錢，來支付這些人的醫療保健費用。

　　直到現在，抽煙一直被認為是一種可接受的消遣。事實上，尼古丁是一種藥物，抽煙的人是會上癮的。有這麼多證據顯示抽煙的害處，下次若有人問：「你介意我抽煙嗎？」我們應該說：「是的，為了你我的健康，我介意。」

**　———————————————————

hazardous〔'hæzɚdəs〕*adj.* 危險的
cancer〔'kænsɚ〕*n.* 癌症　　***as well as*** 以及
passive〔'pæsɪv〕*adj.* 被動的
***passive smoker*** 吸入二手煙的人
statistics〔stə'tɪstɪks〕*n. pl.* 統計數字
***a large number of*** 很多的
***be related to*** 和～有關　　***health care*** 醫療保健
***up to now*** 直到現在　　regard〔rɪ'gɑrd〕*v.* 認為
acceptable〔ək'sɛptəbḷ〕*adj.* 可接受的
pastime〔'pæsˌtaɪm〕*n.* 消遣
nicotine〔'nɪkəˌtin〕*n.* 尼古丁
***be addicted to*** 對～上癮　　evidence〔'ɛvədəns〕*n.* 證據

# 71. The Importance of Being Healthy

It is often said that health is wealth. This suggests that we should aim for health in the same way that many people aim for wealth. *In fact*, the goal of good health is much easier to achieve than that of wealth, since if we start trying to be healthy, the results are immediate and concrete. Money, *meanwhile*, can take a long time to accumulate.

What should we do to stay healthy? We should try to keep healthy both physically and mentally. We should eat good food and get plenty of exercise, and try to broaden our minds and think positively. Being healthy in this way makes our happiness deep and lasting, which helps us and helps others.

# 71. 健康的重要

　　常言道，健康就是財富。這句話意味著，我們應該像許多人追求財富一樣追求健康。事實上，良好健康的目標，要比追求財富容易達成，因爲如果我們開始試著保健，成果是十分迅速而且具體的。然而，金錢可能要花很長的時間才能累積。

　　我們該如何保持健康？我們應該要兼顧身、心兩方面的健康。我們應該吃好的食物、多做運動，而且要拓展心智，並且要有樂觀的想法。身心健康可以使我們擁有極度且持久的快樂，不僅對自己，也對別人有幫助。

**\*\***

wealth〔wɛlθ〕*n.* 財富　　***aim for*** 追求
achieve〔ə'tʃiv〕*v.* 達到
immediate〔ɪ'midɪɪt〕*adj.* 立即的
concrete〔kɑn'krit〕*adj.* 具體的
meanwhile〔'min͵hwaɪl〕*adv.* 另一方面；然而
accumulate〔ə'kjumjə͵let〕*v.* 累積；積蓄
physically〔'fɪzɪkl̩ɪ〕*adv.* 身體上
mentally〔'mɛntl̩ɪ〕*adv.* 心理上
***plenty of*** 很多的　　broaden〔'brɔdn̩〕*v.* 拓展
positively〔'pɑzətɪvlɪ〕*adv.* 積極地
***think positively*** 有樂觀的想法；有自信的想法
deep〔dip〕*adj.* 強烈的；極度的
lasting〔'læstɪŋ〕*adj.* 持久的

# 72. The Person I Admire Most

The person I admire most is my father. He is just and kind and often spends his spare time working for charities and helping other people in the community.

My father works as a policeman. I believe policemen play an important role in society. *They protect our lives and property and they attempt to prevent crime and catch criminals.* Often they must risk their lives in order to do their duty. I am very proud of my father, and I hope that when I grow up I will be just like him.

# 72. 我最敬佩的人

　　我最敬佩的人是我父親。他爲人正直而且仁慈，並且常會利用空閒時間爲慈善機構做事，並幫助社區裡的其他居民。

　　我的父親是個警察。我認爲警察在社會上扮演了十分重要的角色。他們保護我們的生命和財產，並努力防範犯罪及逮捕罪犯。警察常必須冒著生命危險去執行任務。我非常以我的父親爲榮，希望我長大以後也能像他一樣。

\*\* ─────────────────────

　　just〔dʒʌst〕*adj.* 正直的　　*adv.* 的確；完全
　　***spare time*** 空閒時間
　　charity〔'tʃærətɪ〕*n.* 慈善機構
　　community〔kə'mjunətɪ〕*n.* 社區
　　***work as*** 擔任　　　property〔'prɑpətɪ〕*n.* 財產
　　***attempt to V.*** 企圖；嘗試
　　crime〔kraɪm〕*n.* 犯罪行爲
　　criminal〔'krɪmənḷ〕*n.* 罪犯
　　***risk*** *one's* ***life*** 冒生命危險
　　***in order to V.*** 爲了
　　***do*** *one's* ***duty*** 盡職；盡本分　　　***grow up*** 長大

# 73. The Person Who Influenced Me Most

*The person who influenced me most was my English teacher in junior high school.* It was she who first got me interested in English. She taught us through English songs, movies and interesting conversations. Thanks to her, all the students enjoyed English class.

Her greatest gift as a teacher was the ability to make the students enthusiastic. She knew how to make things fun, and she was very patient, which is important in teaching languages. Although I haven't seen her since graduation, her influence on me will last for the rest of my life.

## 73. 影響我最深的人

影響我最深的人，就是我國中時的英文老師。最早就是她使我對英文感興趣。她利用英文歌曲、電影，以及有趣的對話來教導我們。由於她的緣故，所有的學生都很喜歡上英文課。

她當老師最大的天賦，就是能讓學生充滿熱忱。她知道如何使事情變得很有趣，而且她非常有耐心，這在語言教學方面，是非常重要的。儘管自國中畢業後，我就不曾見過她，但她對我的影響，將持續一生。

\*\* ─────────────────────

influence〔ˈɪnfluəns〕*v. n.* 影響

get〔gɛt〕*v.* 使…成為（某種狀態）

through〔θru〕*prep.* 藉由

***thanks to*** 因為；由於    gift〔gɪft〕*n.* 天賦

enthusiastic〔ɪn͵θjuziˈæstɪk〕*adj.* 充滿熱忱的

fun〔fʌn〕*adj.* 有趣的

patient〔ˈpeʃənt〕*adj.* 有耐心的

graduation〔͵grædʒuˈeʃən〕*n.* 畢業

last〔læst〕*v.* 持續

rest〔rɛst〕*n.* 剩餘部份

***the rest of*** *one's life* 餘生

# 74. The Phrase Which Influences Me Most

I used to delay everything until the last minute. My teachers and friends would get annoyed. It seemed that I always had so many things to do that I never knew where to start. I was really confused and I used my time inefficiently.

Then my mother told me, "*Never put off until tomorrow what you can do today*." I took her advice to heart. Now I make a list of things to do each day and do the best I can to get them all done that day. Now I don't have so many things to do and I have more spare time to do what I like. It was really good advice!

## 74. 影響我最深的一句話

我以前常會將每件事情拖延到最後一分鐘。老師和朋友都會很生氣。我似乎總是有很多事情要做，讓我不知從何著手。我覺得十分困惑，而且不會有效率地善用時間。

後來我的母親告訴我說：「今日事，今日畢。」我將她的勸告牢記在心。現在我會列出一張清單，寫出每天要做的事，並且盡力在當天全部做完。現在，我手邊不會有那麼多的事要做，而且也有更多的空閒時間做自己喜歡做的事。這真是一個非常好的勸告！

**

phrase〔frez〕*n.* 片語；名言
***used to*** 以前　　delay〔dɪ'le〕*v.* 拖延
annoyed〔ə'nɔɪd〕*adj.* 生氣的；苦惱的
confused〔kən'fjuzd〕*adj.* 困惑的
inefficiently〔͵ɪnə'fɪʃəntlɪ〕*adv.* 無效率地
***put off*** 拖延
***take～to heart*** 將～牢記在心
advice〔əd'vaɪs〕*n.* 勸告
***do the best*** one *can* 盡力
***spare time*** 空閒時間

# 75. The Pleasure of Helping Others

Everybody needs help sometimes. When we are in need, we turn to others for help. We feel frustrated if we are rejected. ***Therefore***, we should always be willing to help others. Our help, however small it may be, could mean a lot to others.

I once had an especially rewarding experience of helping another person. I helped an old lady pick up her things which she had accidentally dropped on the street while walking. She began to thank me profusely; I was really delighted and touched by her display of gratitude. Now I realize that if we were all willing to help each other, our society would be a warmer and more peaceful place to live in.

# 75. 助人之樂

　　每個人偶爾都需要幫助。當我們有困難時，我們會向別人求助，如果被拒絕，就會覺得很沮喪。因此，我們應該要樂於助人，因為不管我們提供的幫助有多微不足道，對別人來說，可能意義非凡。

　　我曾經有過一次特別有收穫的助人經驗。我幫一位老太太撿起她在街上走路時，無意間掉落的東西。她開始不停地謝我；我真的覺得很高興，而且被她所表達的謝意所感動。現在我終於體會到，如果我們全都樂於相互幫助，我們所居住的社會，將會變成一個更溫馨而且更和平的地方。

**\*\***————————————————————

**in need**　窮困時；有困難時

**turn to** sb. **for help**　向某人求助

frustrated〔'frʌstretɪd〕adj. 受挫的；失望的；沮喪的

reject〔rɪ'dʒɛkt〕v. 拒絕　　willing〔'wɪlɪŋ〕adj. 願意的

however〔hau'ɛvɚ〕adv. 無論多麼地（ = no matter how ）

rewarding〔rɪ'wɔrdɪŋ〕adj. 值得做的；有意義的

accidentally〔͵æksə'dɛntl̩ɪ〕adv. 偶然；意外地

profusely〔prə'fjuslɪ〕adv. 豐富地；不吝惜地

delighted〔dɪ'laɪtɪd〕adj. 高興的

touched〔tʌtʃt〕adj. 感動的　　display〔dɪ'sple〕n. 表露

gratitude〔'grætə͵tjud〕n. 感激

# 76. The Pleasure of Reading

*For me, being without a book is like being a fish out of water.* Reading is not only a pleasure for me, but also a necessity. When I want to educate myself and broaden my horizons, reading books provides the best way to gain knowledge. When I am bored, reading helps to pass the time enjoyably. When I have leisure time, I like to read books.

Of all the various kinds of books, novels are my favorite. Reading a novel is like experiencing things yourself. Different characters present a variety of problems. After seeing how they solve their problems, I often consider whether those same solutions apply to my own difficulties. If sometimes the characters fail, I try to bear that in mind, so that I can avoid making the same mistake. In reading you can learn many lessons.

# 76. 閱讀的樂趣

對我來說，沒有書的生活，就好像魚離開了水一樣。讀書對我而言，不僅是一種樂趣，也是一種需要。當我想要充實自我、拓展眼界時，讀書就是我獲取知識最好的方法。當我感到無聊時，讀書可以幫助我快樂地渡過那段時間。所以當我有空時，我很喜歡讀書。

在各類的書籍中，我最喜歡的是小說。讀小說就像身歷其境一般，不同的角色會產生各式各樣的問題。看著他們如何解決問題之後，我自己也常想，不知道同樣的解決辦法是否也可以用來解決我自己的困難。如果有時候小說裏的人物失敗了，我會盡量牢記在心，如此一來，就可以避免犯同樣的錯誤。從閱讀中我們可以學到許多的教訓。

**\*\***————————————————

necessity〔nə'sɛsətɪ〕*n.* 需要
broaden〔'brɔdn̩〕*v.* 拓展；擴大
horizons〔hə'raɪznz〕*n. pl.* 知識範圍
***broaden one's horizons*** 拓展眼界
enjoyably〔ɪn'dʒɔɪəblɪ〕*adv.* 令人愉快地
***leisure time*** 空閒時間　　various〔'vɛrɪəs〕*adj.* 各種不同的
character〔'kærɪktɚ〕*n.* 人物
present〔prɪ'zɛnt〕*v.* 呈現；引起
***a variety of*** 各種的；各式各樣的
solution〔sə'luʃən〕*n.* 解決之道　　***apply to*** 適用於
***bear~in mind*** 將~牢記在心
***so that*** 以便於　　***learn a lesson*** 學到教訓

# 77. The Cell Phone in Our Daily Lives

Cell phones have many advantages. ***First of all***, they enable us to communicate with each other no matter where we are. There is never a time we are out of reach. ***In addition to this***, cell phones have made it easier to do business. The introduction of smart phones has allowed businessmen to take the office wherever they go. Business can be transacted between several parties without anyone ever meeting face to face; ***instead***, they can send files and contracts in emails.

***Despite its many advantages***, ***the cell phone also has its drawbacks***. Some people have become too dependent on their cell phones. Rather than meeting and talking to their friends in person, they rely on text messages to stay connected. We cannot forget that our electronic devices will never take the place of interpersonal contact. ***Like everything***, ***cell phones should used in moderation***.

# 77. 手機與生活

　　手機有很多優點。首先，無論我們在何處，都能用手機互相連絡，絕不會有失去聯絡的時候。此外，手機使做生意變得更容易。使用智慧型手機，能讓商人把辦公室帶著走。大家不用面對面，就能達成交易，而利用電子郵件，就能傳送檔案和合約。

　　儘管有這許多優點，手機還是有缺點。有些人變得太依賴手機。他們依賴簡訊來保持連絡，而不是親自和朋友見面和交談。我們不能忘記，電子用品絕對無法取代人與人之間的接觸。手機就像其他的東西一樣，應該適度地使用。

\*\* ─────────────────────

*cell phone* 手機 ( = *cellular phone* )
communicate〔kəˋmjunəˎket〕*v.* 溝通；聯繫
*out of reach* 失去連絡 ( = *out of touch* )
introduction〔ˎɪntrəˋdʌkʃən〕*n.* 引進；採用
*smart phone* 智慧型手機　　allow〔əˋlaʊ〕*v.* 讓
transact〔trænˋsækt〕*v.* 進行 ( 交易 )　　party〔ˋpɑrtɪ〕*n.* 一方
*face to face* 面對面　　instead〔ɪnˋstɛd〕*adv.* 取而代之
drawback〔ˋdrɔˎbæk〕*n.* 缺點　　*rather than* 不… ( 而～ )
*in person* 親自　　*text message* 簡訊
connected〔kəˋnɛktɪd〕*adj.* 連接的；有來往的
electronic〔ɪˎlɛkˋtrɑnɪk〕*adj.* 電子的
device〔dɪˋvaɪs〕*n.* 裝置；器具　　*take the place of* 代替
interpersonal〔ˎɪntəˋpɜsn̩l〕*adj.* 人與人之間的
moderation〔ˎmɑdəˋreʃən〕*n.* 節制；適中
*in moderation* 適度地

## 78. Think Before You Speak

Taking care with what we say is obviously very important. Too many people are careless about what they say, so they are often misunderstood, and sometimes they hurt others.

*As the saying goes*, "*The pen is mightier than the sword*." This applies to spoken words also. In some countries, the government is afraid of ordinary people expressing what they think because they might complain and want to change things. Ideally, we should be able to say what we think about the government and our lives, but we should be aware of the effect our words have on other people.

# 78. 三思而後言

　　說話要謹慎，顯然是非常重要的。有很多人不注意自己的言詞，因而常被誤解，有時候也會傷害到別人。

　　俗話說：「文勝於武。」這句話也適用於說話方面。在某些國家，政府很害怕老百姓表達自己的想法，因為他們可能會抱怨，想要改變現況。最理想的狀況是，我們應該都能表達對政府，以及對自己生活的看法，但是我們也應該要注意，自己所說的話可能會對別人造成的影響。

**\*\*** ──────────────

***take care with*** 小心；注意
obviously〔'ɑbvɪəslɪ〕*adv.* 顯然
careless〔'kɛrlɪs〕*adj.* 不小心的；粗心的
misunderstand〔͵mɪsʌndɚ'stænd〕*v.* 誤會
saying〔'seɪŋ〕*n.* 諺語
mighty〔'maɪtɪ〕*adj.* 強大的　　sword〔sɔrd〕*n.* 劍
***The pen is mightier than the sword.***
【諺】筆誅勝於劍伐；文勝於武。
***apply to*** 適用於
ordinary〔'ɔrdn͵ɛrɪ〕*adj.* 普通的；平常的
***ordinary people*** 老百姓
complain〔kəm'plen〕*v.* 抱怨　　things〔θɪŋz〕*n. pl.* 情況
ideally〔aɪ'diəlɪ〕*adv.* 最理想的是
***be aware of*** 知道；察覺到　　effect〔ɪ'fɛkt〕*n.* 影響

# 79. Time

***Lost time is never recovered**, which makes it extremely precious*. There is a saying, "Time is money;" but in my view, time is much more precious than money. If I run out of money, I can earn it again by working hard. ***However***, if I waste my time, I can never get it back. I always try to use time wisely.

I used to waste a lot of time fooling around and daydreaming. In order to stop these bad habits and use my time more efficiently, I came up with an effective method. I make a schedule to arrange my time and keep a record of how I spent it. ***In this way***, I can control the way the precious time passes, and try to make the most of it.

# 79. 時　間

　　失去的時間永遠找不回來，這使得時間異常珍貴。
俗話說：「時間就是金錢。」但在我看來，時間比金錢更
珍貴。如果錢用完了，只要努力工作，就可以再賺回
來。然而，如果浪費了時間，則永遠無法讓時間倒流。
我總是會設法善用時間。

　　從前我常無所事事、做白日夢，因而浪費了許多時
間。爲了擺脫這些壞習慣，並更有效率地利用時間，我
想出了一個有效的方法。我列了一張時間表來安排時
間，並記錄自己是如何使用時間。如此一來，我就可以
掌控所花費的寶貴時間，並盡可能善用時間。

** ————————————————————

recover〔rɪˈkʌvɚ〕*v.* 尋回；恢復
extremely〔ɪkˈstrimlɪ〕*adv.* 非常
saying〔ˈseɪŋ〕*n.* 諺語
precious〔ˈprɛʃəs〕*adj.* 珍貴的
***in my view*** 依我之見　　　***run out of*** 用完
***used to*** 以前　　***fool around*** 無所事事；鬼混
daydream〔ˈdeˌdrim〕*v.* 做白日夢
efficiently〔əˈfɪʃəntlɪ〕*adv.* 有效率地
***come up with*** 想出　　effective〔əˈfɛktɪv〕*adj.* 有效的
schedule〔ˈskɛdʒul〕*n.* 時間表
arrange〔əˈrendʒ〕*v.* 安排　　***keep a record of*** 記錄
***make the most of*** 善加利用

# 80. Traveling

*There is an old Chinese proverb that traveling hundreds of miles is better than reading thousands of books.* We can acquire knowledge by reading books; however, reading books is no substitute for traveling. Not until we experience things for ourselves can we realize what is true or made up. *Besides*, traveling helps people rest and relax.

The place I want to go most is mainland China. I have learned from geography books and travel guides that mainland China is one of the most beautiful places in the world. For years I have planned to go. *Unfortunately*, I still haven't been there. I hope in the future to have a chance to fulfill my dream.

# 80. 旅 行

中國有句俗話說：「行萬里路，勝讀萬卷書。」雖然讀書可以讓我們獲得知識，但卻無法取代旅行。只有在我們自己親身體驗後，才會知道事情究竟是真是假。此外，旅行還可以幫助人們休息與放鬆。

我最想去的地方是中國大陸。根據地理書籍以及旅遊指南上的記載，中國大陸是世界上最美麗的地方之一。多年來，我一直很想去，但遺憾的是，現在我仍然沒去過。希望將來我能有機會實現我的夢想。

**

proverb〔'prɑvɜb〕*n.* 諺語（= *saying*）
acquire〔ə'kwaɪr〕*v.* 獲得
no〔no〕*adv.* 絕不；根本不
substitute〔'sʌbstə,tjut〕*n.* 代替品 < *for* >
***not until*** … 直到…才
experience〔ɪk'spɪrɪəns〕*v.* 經歷；體驗
***for*** oneself 自己　　***make up*** 編造
relax〔rɪ'læks〕*v.* 放鬆
***mainland China*** 中國大陸
geography〔dʒi'ɑgrəfɪ〕*n.* 地理
***travel guide*** 旅遊指南
unfortunately〔ʌn'fɔrtʃənɪtlɪ〕*adv.* 遺憾的是
fulfill〔fʊl'fɪl〕*v.* 實現

# 81. What I Think About Being Overloaded with Schoolwork

I feel that the worst thing about being a student is the amount of schoolwork. Even in elementary school, when we are supposed to play and have fun, we have to do homework after class. In high school, we are never free from the pressure of exams.

I have several suggestions on how to improve our education. *First of all*, some study materials should be improved to cut out the many insignificant things. *Second*, extracurricular activities should be included in our education. Too much work can dull the mind and outside hobbies can increase our happiness and improve our imagination. That should be the goal of general education.

# 81.  我對功課沈重的看法

我覺得身為學生，最糟的就是功課的份量太重。即使是小學，應該要玩樂的時期，上完課後也必寫作業。到了中學時，我們完全擺脫不了考試的壓力。

要如何才能改善我們的教育，我個人有幾點建議。首先，有些課程內容應該要有所改進，刪掉許多不重要的內容。其次，應將課外活動納入正規的教育中。過多的功課可能會使我們的心智遲鈍，而課外的嗜好，卻能使我們更愉快，並增進我們的想像力。這才是通才教育所應達到的目標。

** ————————————————

overload〔'ovɚ,lod〕v. 給…負擔過重
schoolwork〔'skul,wɝk〕n. 功課
**be supposed to**  應該    **be free from**  免於
pressure〔'prɛʃɚ〕n. 壓力
improve〔ɪm'pruv〕v. 改善    **cut out**  刪掉
insignificant〔,ɪnsɪg'nɪfəkənt〕adj. 不重要的
extracurricular〔,ɛkstrəkə'rɪkjələ〕adj. 課外的
dull〔dʌl〕v. 使遲鈍
outside〔'aut'saɪd〕adj. 學業以外的；閒暇的
**general education**  通才教育

# 82. What I Think About the College Entrance Exam

***I think the college entrance exam has more advantages than disadvantages.*** It is a fairer system of examination than the system used in previous times. Those who want to attend college need not worry about their family background or financial status. All they need to do is work hard. As long as they are capable of passing the exam, they can receive a college education.

***In addition***, I believe the exam can be a useful preparation for later life. Students learn how to make good use of their time and to ignore distractions while studying. The college entrance exam thus provides a good opportunity for students to develop patience and perseverance. While not fun, the college entrance exam is an important event in our lives that can help us later with whatever we do.

# 82. 我對大學入學考試的看法

　　我認為大學入學考試的優點比缺點多。這種考試制度比以往的制度更公平。凡是想上大學的人，不需要擔心自己的家庭背景或是財經地位，只要努力就有機會上大學。只要能通過大學入學考試，就能接受大學教育。

　　除此之外，我認為大學入學考試對於日後的生活，是種很有用的準備過程。學生能學會如何善用時間，而且唸書時心無旁騖。因此，大學入學考試能提供學生一個培養耐心與毅力的好機會。雖然大學入學考試並不有趣，但卻是我們人生中十分重要的事件，對我們將來做任何事都很有幫助。

**

---

***the college entrance exam*** 大學入學考試

fair〔fɛr〕*adj.* 公平的　　previous〔'priviəs〕*adj.* 以前的

times〔taɪmz〕*n.* 時代

background〔'bæk,graʊnd〕*n.* 背景

financial〔faɪ'nænʃəl〕*adj.* 財務的

status〔'stetəs〕*n.* 地位；狀況

***all* one *needs to do is V.*** 某人所需要做的就是…

***as long as*** 只要　　***be capable of*** 能夠

receive〔rɪ'siv〕*v.* 得到　　***in addition*** 此外

***make good use of*** 善用　　ignore〔ɪg'nɔr〕*v.* 忽視

distraction〔dɪ'strækʃən〕*n.* 使人分心的事物

thus〔ðʌs〕*adv.* 因此　　develop〔dɪ'vɛləp〕*v.* 培養

perseverance〔,pɝsə'vɪrəns〕*n.* 毅力

***While not fun,* ...** 雖然並不有趣，…（*= While it is not fun, ...*）

event〔ɪ'vɛnt〕*n.* 事件；大型活動

## 83. What I Value Most in a Good Friend

No one is an island entirely isolated from society, and people cannot live happily without friends. When we are in difficulty, good friends will come to our help. When we feel blue, good friends will stand by us and comfort us. When we are happy, friends can share our happiness.

***The qualities I value most in a good friend are sincerity and a sense of humor***. A sincere person will not cheat or lie. He will always be frank and upright, and a person can depend on him. Humorous people always see the bright side of things because of their positive philosophy of life, which can also help us to feel better. I think sincerity and a sense of humor are the most important qualities that a good friend should have.

## 83. 好友所應具備的重要特質

　　沒有人能夠成為和社會完全隔離的孤島，沒有朋友的人，無法生活得很愉快。當我們有困難時，好朋友會對我們伸出援手。當我們覺得憂鬱的時候，好朋友會支持並安慰我們。當我們快樂的時候，朋友可以分享我們的喜悅。

　　好友所應具備的特質中，我最重視的是誠懇和幽默感。真誠的人不會欺騙或說謊。真誠的人總是坦白又正直，能讓人信賴。幽默的人總是看到事情的光明面，因為他們具有積極的人生觀，能幫助我們覺得更愉快。我認為誠懇和幽默感，是好朋友所應具備最重要的特質。

**\*\*** ─────────────────────

value〔ˋvæljʊ〕v. 重視　　isolate〔ˋaɪsḷ͵et〕v. 使隔離
**come to one's help**　前來幫忙某人
blue〔blu〕adj. 憂鬱的　　**stand by sb.**　支持某人
comfort〔ˋkʌmfət〕v. 安慰
share〔ʃɛr〕v. 分享　　quality〔ˋkwɑlətɪ〕n. 特質
sincerity〔sɪnˋsɛrətɪ〕n. 誠懇　　humor〔ˋhjumə〕n. 幽默
**a sense of humor**　幽默感　　sincere〔sɪnˋsɪr〕adj. 真誠的
frank〔fræŋk〕adj. 坦白的
upright〔ˋʌp͵raɪt〕adj. 正直的
**see the bright side of things**　看事情的光明面；
　抱持樂觀的態度
positive〔ˋpɑzətɪv〕adj. 積極的；樂觀的
**philosophy of life**　人生觀

## 84. What I Want to Do Most After the College Entrance Exam

For most students, finishing the college entrance exam is like being relieved of a burden. The college entrance exam puts an end to three years of suffering from staying up late at night cramming. Upon finishing the exam, *some* people want to celebrate; *others* just want to get a good night's sleep; *still others* just want to relax and take time to do what they like.

When I complete the exam, what I want to do most is to reflect on the past three years. It's a chance to examine carefully what I have gained or lost. I would also like to note down what I failed to do in senior high school and try to achieve it in college. I want to prepare myself for a more varied life after the college entrance exam.

# 84. 大學入學考試後我最想做的事

對於大多數的學生而言，考完大學入學考試，眞是如釋重負。大學入學考試結束了考生三年來，每晚熬夜 K 書的痛苦。一考完試，有些人想大肆慶祝，而有些人則是想好好地睡一覺，還有些人則是想要放輕鬆，花點時間做自己想做的事。

當我考完大學入學考試之後，最想做的，就是回顧過去這三年。這是個可以仔細反省自己的得與失的機會。我也想要寫下在高中生活中，沒有辦法做的事，試著上大學之後來完成。我想讓自己爲大學入學考試之後，更多彩多姿的生活做好準備。

\*\* —————————————————

relieve〔rɪˈliv〕*v.* 使減輕

***be relieved of*** 擺脫；免除　　 burden〔ˈbɝdn̩〕*n.* 負擔

***put an end to*** 結束　　***suffer from*** 因…而受苦

***stay up*** 熬夜　　 cram〔kræm〕*v.* K 書；死記

***upon + V-ing*** 一…就（= *on + V-ing = as soon as +* 子句）

***some…others…still others*** 有些…有些…還有一些

***take time*** 花時間　　 complete〔kəmˈplit〕*v.* 完成

reflect〔rɪˈflɛkt〕*v.* 反省 < *on* >

examine〔ɪgˈzæmɪn〕*v.* 仔細檢查

gain〔gen〕*v.* 獲得　　***note down*** 記下

***fail to V.*** 無法～　　 achieve〔əˈtʃiv〕*v.* 完成；實現

varied〔ˈvɛrɪd〕*adj.* 富於變化的；多彩多姿的

# 85. What I Want to Major in in College

My plans for college are to major in literature, both Chinese and English. Being Chinese, I deem it necessary to have a good understanding of Chinese literature. Although we are exposed to this language all the time, most of us are not proficient in it. Majoring in Chinese literature would give me great insight into my own language.

English has become the world's most popular language. ***English can help both at work and while traveling***. That is my main reason for studying it. ***Of course***, another reason is, I admit, that I am afraid of mathematics. Literature can take me away from those confusing math problems. I look forward to studying literature for all these reasons.

## 85. 上大學時我想就讀的科系

　　我打算上大學時，主修中國文學和英國文學。我認為身為中國人，就必須非常了解中國文學。雖然我們一直在接觸中文，但我們大部份的人對中文並不精通。主修中國文學，能使我對自己的語言有更深入的了解。

　　英語已成為全球最通行的語言。英語在工作及旅遊時，都很有用處，這是我想研讀英語的主要原因。當然，我承認，另一個原因是因為我害怕數學。文學可以使我擺脫惱人的數學題目。因為這些原因，我非常期待自己能研讀文學。

**　────────────────

　major〔'medʒɚ〕*v.* 主修 < *in* >　*n.* 主修科目
　deem〔dim〕*v.* 認為
　***have a good understanding of*** 非常了解
　***be exposed to*** 接觸　　***all the time*** 一直
　proficient〔prə'fɪʃənt〕*adj.* 精通的 < *in* >
　insight〔'ɪn,saɪt〕*n.* 洞察（力）；頓悟
　***have great insight into*** 非常了解
　help〔hɛlp〕*v.* 有幫助；有用
　confusing〔kən'fjuzɪŋ〕*adj.* 令人困惑的
　***look forward to*** 期待

# 86. What Is Happiness?

Happiness is being free from worry. That is not, ***however***, the same as being able to do anything you want. Doing something and enjoying it simply for itself brings happiness. When children play, they do not worry about other things. For adults, pleasure is more difficult to find.

I often find pleasure in reading novels. When I am reading, I not only obtain knowledge, but also forget my troubles. I become lost in the world of the author. I laugh at the comedy, and I cry at the tragedy. I always resort to books when I am depressed, because I can derive happiness from reading.

# 86. 快樂是什麼？

快樂就是無憂無慮。然而，這和隨心所欲不同。做某件事，並且很喜歡做，就能帶來快樂。小孩在玩的時候，不會煩惱其他的事情。至於成人，要快樂就比較困難了。

看小說常使我覺得樂趣無窮。讀書不僅能使我獲得知識，也能讓我忘記煩惱。我會沈浸在作者的世界裏，因爲喜劇而笑，也會因爲悲劇而流淚。心情沮喪時，我一定會讀書，因爲我能從閱讀中得到快樂。

\*\*———————————————

**be free from** 擺脫；免於
pleasure〔'plɛʒɚ〕*n.* 樂趣
**not only…but also** 不僅…而且
obtain〔əb'ten〕*v.* 獲得
troubles〔'trʌblz〕*n. pl.* 煩惱
**be lost in** 沈浸於  author〔'ɔθɚ〕*n.* 作者
comedy〔'kɑmədɪ〕*n.* 喜劇
tragedy〔'trædʒədɪ〕*n.* 悲劇
**resort to** 依靠；訴諸於
depressed〔dɪ'prɛst〕*adj.* 沮喪的
derive〔də'raɪv〕*v.* 獲得

## 87. What Makes a Good Teacher

*In my opinion*, a good teacher is more than an instructor. A teacher is someone who passes down knowledge to students, but also a good friend who is willing to offer a hand. *Therefore*, a good teacher must have enthusiasm and patience.

An enthusiastic teacher will have an optimistic attitude. His enthusiasm for the subject is recognized by his students. Patience is necessary for making sure the students are following the new ideas the teacher is introducing. Some students are slow or unsure of themselves and so a teacher must be particularly understanding towards them. These are just two of the many requirements for a teacher, but I think they are the most important.

## 87. 好老師所應具備的條件

依我之見，一位好老師，不只是老師。好老師會把知識傳授給學生，而且也是個樂於幫助學生的好朋友。因此，好老師必須要有熱忱和耐心。

一位有熱忱的老師，會抱持著樂觀的態度。他對於該科目的熱忱，會受到學生的認同。老師必須要有耐心，才能確定學生是否已完全了解所介紹的新概念。有些學生反應較慢，或對自己較沒自信，所以對於這些學生，老師應該要特別體諒他們。這只是好老師所應具備的許多必要條件中的兩項，但是我認為，這兩項是最重要的。

\*\* —————————————————————

instructor〔ɪnˋstrʌktɚ〕*n.* 教師
***pass down A to B*** 把 A 傳給 B
willing〔ˋwɪlɪŋ〕*adj.* 願意的　　***offer a hand*** 幫忙
enthusiasm〔ɪnˋθjuzɪˏæzəm〕*n.* 熱忱
patience〔ˋpeʃəns〕*n.* 耐心
enthusiastic〔ɪnˏθjuzɪˋæstɪk〕*adj.* 熱心的
optimistic〔ˏɑptəˋmɪstɪk〕*adj.* 樂觀的
recognize〔ˋrɛkəɡˏnaɪz〕*v.* 認可
follow〔ˋfalo〕*v.* 能聽懂　　slow〔slo〕*adj.* 遲鈍的
unsure〔ʌnˋʃur〕*adj.* 無自信的＜*of*＞
understanding〔ˏʌndɚˋstændɪŋ〕*adj.* 體諒的
requirement〔rɪˋkwaɪrmənt〕*n.* 必備條件

# 88. Why I Don't Want to Study Abroad

The number of students studying abroad has been on the increase in recent years. Students go abroad for various reasons. *Some* favor the Western educational system. *Others* hope for a new experience in life. *Still others* think that the grass is always greener on the other side of the fence.

*However*, for my part, I don't intend to go abroad after graduation. It is not easy to get used to the life and weather elsewhere. Perhaps there would be a problem in communicating and getting on with the local people. Perhaps I would simply be homesick. All these factors might affect my studies, which should be my priority. The facilities in Taiwan are certainly good enough for me. Why spend so much money to go abroad?

# 88. 我為什麼不想出國留學

　　近年來，出國留學的學生人數不斷增加。學生想出國的理由有很多。有些學生比較喜歡西方的教育制度，有些則是希望能有新的生活經驗，還有些人認為外國的月亮比較圓。

　　然而，就我而言，我畢業後並不打算出國。要適應外地的生活和天氣並不容易，也許和當地居民在溝通和相處方面，可能會有困難。我也可能會想家。這些因素都可能會影響我的學業，而學業應該是我必須優先考慮的事。台灣的教育設施對我來說已經夠好了，為什麼要花這麼多錢出國呢？

\*\* ——————————————————

abroad〔əˋbrɔd〕*adv.* 在國外　　increase〔ˋɪnkris〕*n.* 增加
***on the increase*** 在增加中
***some…others…still others*** 有些…有些…還有一些
favor〔ˋfevɚ〕*v.* 偏愛　　***hope for*** 期望；期待
grass〔græs〕*n.* 草　　fence〔fɛns〕*n.* 籬笆
***The grass is always greener on the other side of the fence.***
【諺】鄰家芳草綠，隔岸風景好；外國的月亮比較圓。
***for*** one's ***part*** 就某人而言　　***intend to V.*** 打算
***get used to*** 習慣於　　elsewhere〔ˋɛls͵hwɛr〕*adv.* 在別處
***get on with*** 和…相處　　local〔ˋlokḷ〕*adj.* 當地的
homesick〔ˋhom͵sɪk〕*adj.* 想家的　　factor〔ˋfæktɚ〕*n.* 因素
affect〔əˋfɛkt〕*v.* 影響
priority〔praɪˋɔrətɪ〕*n.* 優先的事物
facilities〔fəˋsɪlətɪz〕*n. pl.* 設施

# 89. Why I Want to Attend College

Most people go to university to pursue their interests. Others go to receive training and qualifications. ***My main reason for attending college is to pursue knowledge***. A university is a place which provides us with a good study environment. We can further study our interests and sample other subjects, too. ***Thus*** we can find what it is that we are truly interested in.

Friendship is also something that I want to pursue. I like making friends very much and I am sure that I can find many friends in college. ***Different friends bring different experiences and points of view***. I think these are two good goals to pursue, and so I will have to study hard to enter university.

## 89. 我爲什麼要上大學

大多數的人上大學，是爲了追求自己的興趣。而有些人，則是爲了接受訓練，與獲得學位。而我上大學最主要的原因，是想要追求知識。大學能提供給我們良好的讀書環境。我們可以更進一步研讀自己有興趣的科目，也可選修其他科目。如此一來，我們就可以了解自己眞正感興趣的是什麼。

友誼也是我上大學之後想追求的。我非常喜歡交朋友，而且我確定自己可以在大學裏找到許多朋友。不同的朋友能帶給我不同的經驗和觀點。我認爲這是兩個值得努力追求的好目標，所以我必須努力用功，考上大學。

**＊＊**

*attend*
*go to* ｝｛ *college*　上大學
*enter* 　 *university*

pursue〔pɚˋsu〕*v.* 追求　　receive〔rɪˋsiv〕*v.* 得到
qualifications〔͵kwɑləfəˋkeʃənz〕*n. pl.* 學位；文憑
further〔ˋfɝðɚ〕*adv.* 更進一步地
sample〔ˋsæmpḷ〕*v.* 嚐試；體驗
thus〔ðʌs〕*adv.* 因此　　*make friends* 交朋友
*point of view* 觀點　　goal〔gol〕*n.* 目標

# 90. Acid Rain

Our environment has suffered from the effects of acid rain. All you have to do is look at the paint peeling off the surfaces of buildings to know the damage it has done. Regular exposure to acid rain has also interfered with the growth of many plants and animals.

*We must take steps to control this problem.* Acid rain is caused by air pollution, so factories should introduce new equipment to avoid emitting so many chemicals. The emissions of vehicles should also be controlled and new "clean" technology ought to be developed. Only if we make such efforts will the air become clean again.

# 90. 酸　雨

　　我們的環境因酸雨所產生的影響而受到損害。你只要看看建築物表面脫落的油漆，就可以知道酸雨造成的傷害有多大。經常接觸酸雨，也會妨礙許多動植物的生長。

　　要控制酸雨，我們必須採取一些措施。酸雨是由空氣污染所造成的，所以工廠應該引進新的設備，以避免排放過多的化學物質。車輛的排放物也應加以管制，而且必須發展新的「無污染的」技術。唯有做這方面的努力，空氣才能恢復原有的潔淨。

\*\* ————————————————

acid〔'æsɪd〕*adj.* 酸的　　***acid rain*** 酸雨
***all one has to do is V.*** 某人所必須要做的就是
paint〔pent〕*n.* 油漆　　peel〔pil〕*v.* 剝落
***peel off*** 從…剝落　　surface〔'sɝfɪs〕*n.* 表面
regular〔'rɛgjələ〕*adj.* 定期的；經常的
exposure〔ɪk'spoʒə〕*n.* 暴露；接觸 < *to* >
interfere〔ˌɪntə'fɪr〕*v.* 妨礙 < *with* >
step〔stɛp〕*n.* 步驟；措施
introduce〔ˌɪntrə'djus〕*v.* 引進　　emit〔ɪ'mɪt〕*v.* 排放
chemical〔'kɛmɪkḷ〕*n.* 化學物質
emission〔ɪ'mɪʃən〕*n.* 放射物
vehicle〔'viɪkḷ〕*n.* 車輛　　***make efforts*** 努力

# 91. Energy Conservation

Modern life depends on energy. Without energy, our system of transportation could not function. Without power we could not light our houses or preserve food in the refrigerator. *However*, all this energy use has caused a major problem for the future. By using energy too wastefully and irresponsibly, we have created huge environmental problems. We have also used up too much of some nonrenewable resources, such as oil.

Scientists are playing a vital role in conservation by developing new sources of energy. *However*, we too must play our part. If possible, we should take public transport instead of private cars; when we leave the house we should turn off all lights and air-conditioners, etc. *Energy conservation is really something we all must strive for*.

# 91. 節約能源

現代的生活十分依賴能源。如果沒有能源，我們的交通運輸系統將無法運作。如果沒有電力，我們的房子就沒有照明設備，也無法在冰箱中保存食物。然而，我們對能源的使用，已對未來造成了很大的問題。由於我們使用能源時，太過浪費又不負責任，所以已經引起嚴重的環境問題。我們也已經用完太多不可更新的資源，例如石油。

科學家在資源的維護方面，扮演了十分重要的角色，他們會研發新的能源。然而，我們也應該盡自己的本分。如果可能的話，我們應搭乘大眾運輸工具，而不要自己開車；離開家時，應該要關掉所有的電燈及冷氣等等。節約能源真的是一件我們大家必須共同努力的事。

\*\* ─────────────────────

conservation〔ˌkɑnsɚˈveʃən〕*n.* ( 資源的 ) 維護；保存；節省
***depend on*** 依賴    function〔ˈfʌŋkʃən〕*v.* 運作
power〔ˈpauɚ〕*n.* 電力    light〔laɪt〕*v.* 點亮；使明亮
preserve〔prɪˈzɝv〕*v.* 保存
major〔ˈmedʒɚ〕*adj.* 重大的；嚴重的
huge〔hjudʒ〕*adj.* 巨大的    ***use up*** 用完
nonrenewable〔ˌnɑnrɪˈnjuəbļ〕*adj.* 不可更新的
resources〔rɪˈsorsɪz〕*n. pl.* 資源
vital〔ˈvaɪtļ〕*adj.* 極重要的    develop〔dɪˈvɛləp〕*v.* 研發
***source of energy*** 能源    ***play*** *one's* ***part*** 盡本分
transport〔ˈtrænsport〕*n.* 交通工具 ( = *transportation* )
strive〔straɪv〕*v.* 努力

# 92. Our Environment

There are plenty of resources on this planet and they can help to make our lives rich. We have green plants, clear streams, blue skies, and fresh air to use and admire. ***In the past***, we took it for granted that everything was put there for us to use. ***However***, as the years have passed by, we have seen the result of our actions from the poisoning and partial destruction of our natural environment.

***We must take action to prevent our environment from being further destroyed***. ***First of all***, we have to learn much more about environmental protection. We must ***then*** use this knowledge to help to protect our environment. Perhaps then we can make a better tomorrow.

# 92. 我們的環境

地球上有許多資源，幫助我們過著富裕的生活。我們有綠色的植物、清澈的溪流、湛藍的天空，以及新鮮的空氣，可以使用或欣賞。在過去，我們認爲每樣東西就在那裏供我們使用，是理所當然的。然而，這些年來，大家都已經看到我們毒害以及局部破壞自然環境的行爲所造成的結果。

我們必須採取行動，避免環境受到更進一步的破壞。首先，我們必須學習更多環保的知識，並善用這些知識來幫忙保護我們的環境。也許如此我們才能創造一個更美好的明天。

\*\* ─────────────────────

***plenty of*** 很多的

resources〔rɪ'sorsɪz〕*n. pl.* 資源

planet〔'plænɪt〕*n.* 行星【在此指「地球」】

clear〔klɪr〕*adj.* 清澈的　　stream〔strim〕*n.* 小溪

***take it for granted that***~ 把~視爲理所當然

poison〔'pɔɪzn̩〕*v.* 毒害

partial〔'parʃəl〕*adj.* 局部的

destruction〔dɪ'strʌkʃən〕*n.* 破壞

***take action*** 採取行動

further〔'fɜðɚ〕*adv.* 更進一步地

## 93. Protecting Wildlife

As a mountainous island in the subtropical zone, Taiwan is home to many rare wild animals. *In the past*, these wild animals provided food for people living in the mountains. With increasing hunting *in recent years*, some of these animal species have been endangered. To protect them, we must take certain steps.

*Firstly*, the public needs to be educated about the necessity of conservation. The authorities concerned should enforce the laws more strictly to prevent illegal hunting. *Finally*, people living in country areas should help the police by reporting suspicious activities.

# 93. 保護野生動物

　　台灣是位於亞熱帶地區的一座多山的島嶼，有許多稀有的野生動物。以前，這些野生動物提供山區居民食物。近年來，由於狩獵活動日益頻繁，有些種類的動物已經瀕臨絕種。爲了保護這些動物，我們必須採取某些措施。

　　首先，應該要教育一般大衆，保護野生動物的必要。有關當局應該要更嚴格地執行法律，以防止非法狩獵。最後，住在鄉村地區的人，若發現可疑的活動時，應向警方報案。

** ─────────────────────────

wildlife〔'waɪld,laɪf〕*n.* 野生動物
mountainous〔'mauntṇəs〕*adj.* 多山的
subtropical〔sʌb'trɑpɪkḷ〕*adj.* 亞熱帶的
zone〔zon〕*n.* 地區　　　***be home to*** 是～的所在地
rare〔rɛr〕*adj.* 稀有的　　species〔'spiʃɪz〕*n.* 物種
endangered〔ɪn'dendʒəd〕*adj.* 瀕臨絕種的
certain〔'sɝtṇ〕*adj.* 某些
conservation〔,kɑnsə'veʃən〕*n.* （動植物、森林的）保護
***the authorities concerned*** 有關當局
enforce〔ɪn'fors〕*v.* 執行　　strictly〔'strɪktlɪ〕*adv.* 嚴格地
illegal〔ɪ'ligḷ〕*adj.* 非法的
country〔'kʌntrɪ〕*adj.* 鄉村的
suspicious〔sə'spɪʃəs〕*adj.* 可疑的

**94. The Importance of Trees**

*It goes without saying that trees are vital to our daily lives*. They purify our air and produce oxygen for us to breathe. They protect us from floods and droughts by conserving the soil, and stop it from sliding down into the rivers. Their lumber provides material for our furniture, and they also beautify the environment with their greenery.

*However*, despite their importance, trees are rapidly declining in number. Many are being cut down illegally by logging companies. To stop this, violators should be punished, and the authorities concerned should plant trees regularly to maintain their number. *Last but not least, everyone should shoulder the responsibility of protecting trees because this requires everyone's effort.*

# 94. 樹木的重要

　　不用說，樹木對我們日常生活而言，是十分重要的。樹木能淨化空氣，並製造氧氣供我們呼吸，也能保護土壤，使土壤不會滑入河川，讓我們免於洪水和旱災。木材能提供我們製造傢俱的材料，翠綠的樹木也能美化環境。

　　然而，儘管樹木十分重要，其數量卻正急遽減少中。許多樹木正遭到伐木公司非法砍伐。為了制止這種行為，違法者應受到懲罰，而有關當局也應該定期種樹，以維持其數量。最後一項要點是，人人都應肩負起保護樹木的責任，因為這項工作需要大家共同努力。

**

***it goes without saying that*** 不用說
vital〔'vaɪtḷ〕*adj.* 非常重要的　　purify〔'pjʊrə,faɪ〕*v.* 淨化
oxygen〔'ɑksədʒən〕*n.* 氧氣　　flood〔flʌd〕*n.* 水災
drought〔draʊt〕*n.* 旱災　　conserve〔kən'sɝv〕*v.* 保護
soil〔sɔɪl〕*n.* 土壤　　slide〔slaɪd〕*v.* 滑
lumber〔'lʌmbɚ〕*n.* 木材　　beautify〔'bjutə,faɪ〕*v.* 美化
greenery〔'grinərɪ〕*n.* 綠樹；綠葉
rapidly〔'ræpɪdlɪ〕*adv.* 快速地　　decline〔dɪ'klaɪn〕*v.* 減少
log〔lɔg〕*v.* 伐（木）　　violator〔'vaɪə,letɚ〕*n.* 違反者
***the authorities concerned*** 有關當局
regularly〔'rɛgjələlɪ〕*adv.* 定期地
***last but not least*** 最後一項要點是
shoulder〔'ʃoldɚ〕*v.* 負擔；擔當（責任）
require〔rɪ'kwaɪr〕*v.* 需要

## 95. Water

Water is essential to life. We cannot live without water. We have to drink water every day for our bodies to function. As for plants and animals, they also need water to grow. Water can also help to clean our environment and make everything look more beautiful.

Despite water's importance, ***however***, people still carelessly pollute it. There are things we can do to help. ***For example***, we should not throw garbage into the rivers. The government should enforce strict laws to punish those who pollute rivers. With continuous efforts from the citizens as well as the government, our water could become clean again.

# 95. 水

水是維持生命所不可或缺的。我們不能沒有水。
我們必須每天喝水，才能維持身體的正常機能。至於
動植物，它們也需要有水才能生長。水也能用來清理
我們的環境，使每樣東西看起來更美麗。

雖然水是如此重要，人們仍然會任意污染水源。
我們應該想辦法來幫忙改善這種情況。例如，我們不
應該把垃圾丟進河裏。政府應該執行嚴格的法律，來
懲罰那些污染河川的人。唯有民眾與政府持續地努
力，我們的水才能恢復以往的潔淨。

**\*\*** ─────────────────────

essential〔ə'sɛnʃəl〕*adj.* 必要的；不可或缺的
***cannot live without*** 不能沒有
function〔'fʌŋkʃən〕*v.* 起作用；運作
***as for*** 至於　　despite〔dɪ'spaɪt〕*prep.* 儘管
pollute〔pə'lut〕*v.* 污染
garbage〔'gɑrbɪdʒ〕*n.* 垃圾
enforce〔ɪn'fors〕*v.* 執行
strict〔strɪkt〕*adj.* 嚴格的
continuous〔kən'tɪnjʊəs〕*adj.* 連續的；不斷的
citizen〔'sɪtəzn̩〕*n.* 人民　　***as well as*** 以及

## 96. Our Lives with TV

Television has become a must in modern life. Television keeps us informed of what is happening in the world when we watch news programs. It educates us with various documentaries. It may keep us happy with a variety of entertainment programs. *And even commercials keep us up to date with the latest products and trends*.

*Despite the advantages of television, there are many disadvantages*. People spend too much time watching TV, which is a passive activity. Students take time away from their studies to watch it. People in general watch it when they don't have anything better to do. *In reality*, there are very few quality programs. We really should try to select the programs we watch on TV.

# 96. 電視與生活

　　電視已成為現代生活的必需品。當我們收看新聞節目時，電視使我們知道世界各地發生了什麼事。電視利用各式各樣的紀錄片來教育我們。它也藉由各種娛樂節目，使我們快樂。甚至電視上的廣告，也讓我們知道最新的產品和流行趨勢。

　　儘管電視有這些優點，它的缺點也不少。人們花太多時間在看電視這種消極的活動上。學生把許多應該用來讀書的時間，拿來看電視。一般大眾如果沒有更好的事情可做時，就會看電視。事實上，品質好的節目非常少。我們實在應該要好好選擇我們所觀賞的電視節目。

**　——————————————————

　　must〔mʌst〕*n.* 必需品；必備之物
　　inform〔ɪnˈfɔrm〕*v.* 告知；通知
　　***keep sb. informed of*** 隨時告訴某人～
　　various〔ˈvɛrɪəs〕*adj.* 各種不同的
　　documentary〔ˌdɑkjəˈmɛntərɪ〕*n.* 紀錄片
　　***a variety of*** 各種的；各式各樣的
　　commercial〔kəˈmɝʃəl〕*n.* (電視)廣告
　　***up to date with*** 熟知～的資料
　　latest〔ˈletɪst〕*adj.* 最新的　　trend〔trɛnd〕*n.* 趨勢
　　despite〔dɪˈspaɪt〕*prep.* 儘管
　　passive〔ˈpæsɪv〕*adj.* 消極的　　***people in general*** 一般人
　　***in reality*** 事實上 ( = *in fact* )
　　quality〔ˈkwɑlətɪ〕*adj.* 品質好的

# 97. Riding a Motorcycle

I often see accidents involving motorcycles in Taiwan. In most cases the person on the motorcycle was not wearing a helmet, and so was often seriously injured. Now the government is making the wearing of helmets mandatory in order to cut down on serious accidents.

*However*, there are many other reasons why there are so many serious accidents. Perhaps the most obvious reason is the large number of illegal underage riders. Such youths often ride poorly and recklessly, and so many accidents result. *Nevertheless*, these young riders claim that public transportation is so slow that they must ride a motorcycle in order to get to work or to school on time. Maybe our government should make allowance for them and consider lowering the riding age to sixteen as it is in many other countries.

# 97. 騎機車

在台灣，我常看到機車出車禍。通常出車禍的機車騎士都沒戴安全帽，所以常會受重傷。現在政府已經規定，騎機車一定要戴安全帽，以減少嚴重的車禍。

然而，嚴重的車禍如此之多，也有很多其他的原因。也許最明顯的原因，就是有許多未滿十八歲的人違規騎機車。這些年輕人通常騎車技術很差，而且常常橫衝直撞，因而發生許多車禍。然而，這些年輕的機車騎士卻說，由於大眾運輸工具速度十分緩慢，所以他們必須騎機車，以準時上班或上學。也許我們的政府應該體諒他們，考慮和其他許多國家一樣，將騎機車的法定年齡降低為十六歲。

**

involve〔ɪn'vɑlv〕v. 和～有關　　case〔kes〕n. 情況
helmet〔'hɛlmɪt〕n. 安全帽　　injure〔'ɪndʒɚ〕v. 傷害
mandatory〔'mændə,torɪ〕adj. 義務性的；強制的
***cut down on*** 減少　　obvious〔'ɑbvɪəs〕adj. 明顯的
illegal〔ɪ'ligl̩〕adj. 非法的
underage〔'ʌndɚ'edʒ〕adj. 未達法定年齡的
youth〔juθ〕n. 年輕人　　recklessly〔'rɛklɪslɪ〕adv. 魯莽地
result〔rɪ'zʌlt〕v. 產生
nevertheless〔,nɛvɚðə'lɛs〕adv. 然而
claim〔klem〕v. 宣稱
***public transportation*** 大眾運輸工具
***make allowance for*** 體諒；考慮到　　lower〔'loɚ〕v. 降低

## 98. Taking the MRT

Taking the MRT is great. It's very clean and efficient. People are very orderly and it's always on time. *What's more*, the MRT is very affordable. You can go from one side of town to the other for very little money. The MRT makes city life very convenient. You don't have to worry about traffic or parking. You can sit back and enjoy the ride. *I can't imagine life without the MRT*.

In addition to all these advantages, the MRT is also good for the environment. Instead of driving cars and motorcycles, people take the MRT to school and work. That cuts down on air pollution as well as gasoline consumption. *By taking the MRT you are helping to keep our city clean while doing your part to preserve natural resources*. It's a win-win situation. Every city should have such a system.

# 98. 搭捷運

　　搭捷運很棒。捷運非常乾淨，而且很有效率。乘客都很守秩序，而且捷運總是很準時。此外，捷運的車資大家都負擔得起。只要花很少的錢，就可以從城裡的一邊到另一邊。捷運使都市生活變得非常方便，你不需要擔心交通狀況或停車問題。你可以靠著椅背坐，享受搭乘的樂趣。我無法想像沒有捷運的生活。

　　除了上述的優點之外，捷運也對環境有益。大家搭捷運上班和上學，而不是開車或騎摩托車，可以減少空氣污染，以及汽油的消耗量。藉由搭捷運，可以協助保持都市的清潔，同時又盡了保護天然資源的本分。這是個雙贏的局面。每個城市都應該要有捷運系統。

**

efficient〔ə'fɪʃənt〕*adj.* 有效率的
orderly〔'ɔrdəˑlɪ〕*adj.* 井然有序的　　*on time* 準時
parking〔'pɑrkɪŋ〕*n.* 停車
affordable〔ə'fɔrdəbl〕*adj.* 負擔得起的
*sit back* 靠椅背而坐　　*instead of* 不…（而～）
*cut down on* 減少　　*as well as* 以及
gasoline〔'gæslˌin〕*n.* 汽油
consumption〔kən'sʌmpʃən〕*n.* 消耗
while〔hwaɪl〕*conj.* 同時　　*do one's part* 盡自己的本分
preserve〔prɪ'zɝv〕*v.* 保存；保護
*natural resources* 天然資源
*a win-win situation* 雙贏的局面

## 99. Traffic Jams

Unfortunately, Taipei traffic usually moves very slow and is often jammed. Traffic jams put everyone in a bad mood and waste everyone's time. The time everyone spends stuck in traffic could have been spent working and so represents a huge economic loss.

*In my opinion*, the government should further develop the public transportation network to alleviate the congestion. *In the meantime*, drivers and passengers should try to be patient. When I ride on a bus and get caught in a traffic jam, I often listen to music and close my eyes, which relaxes me. Sometimes I even take a nap which refreshes me. Even though it's a bad situation, I try to make the best of it.

# 99. 交通阻塞

　　很遺憾的是，台北的車輛通常移動得十分緩慢，而且常常塞車。塞車不僅會使人心情不好，也浪費大家的時間。花在塞車的時間，原本可以用來工作，所以這就表示塞車會造成我們龐大的經濟損失。

　　依我之見，政府應該更進一步地發展大眾運輸的網路，以減少塞車。同時，駕駛人與乘客都應該要很有耐心。當我搭公車遇上交通阻塞時，我常會閉著眼睛聽音樂，讓自己放鬆一下。有時我甚至會小睡片刻，使自己恢復精神。雖然塞車的情況很糟，我還是會儘量善用這段塞車的時間。

**

jam〔dʒæm〕*n.* 阻塞　*v.* 使阻塞
unfortunately〔ʌnˈfɔrtʃənɪtlɪ〕*adv.* 不幸地；遺憾地
traffic〔ˈtræfɪk〕*n.* 交通；車輛【集合名詞】
*put sb. in a bad mood* 使某人心情不好
stuck〔stʌk〕*adj.* 動彈不得的；困住的
represent〔ˌrɛprɪˈzɛnt〕*v.* 代表；表示
huge〔hjudʒ〕*adj.* 巨大的　　economic〔ˌikəˈnɑmɪk〕*adj.* 經濟的
further〔ˈfɝðɚ〕*adv.* 更進一步地
network〔ˈnɛtˌwɝk〕*n.* 網路
alleviate〔əˈlivɪˌet〕*v.* 減輕；緩和
congestion〔kənˈdʒɛstʃən〕*n.* 阻塞
*in the meantime* 同時　　patient〔ˈpeʃənt〕*adj.* 有耐心的
*get caught in* 遇到　　*take a nap* 小睡片刻
refresh〔rɪˈfrɛʃ〕*v.* 使恢復精神　　*make the best of* 善加利用

# 100. Waiting for a Bus

Waiting for the bus is boring, but as with many things in life, we have no choice. My school is far from where I live, so I cannot walk there. The bus is the most economical and convenient way to travel, so I ride it five days a week. Waiting for a bus that never comes on time is even more frustrating. We need to prepare for the boredom of waiting for the bus.

I always try to find something to do to fight the boredom when I'm waiting. ***Often***, I bring along vocabulary cards to study English words. ***In this way***, I have improved my vocabulary a great deal. If I'm not busy with schoolwork, I like to examine my own behavior to see what is good and what needs improving. Then when the bus comes, once again I can go to school better prepared.

# 100. 等公車

　　等公車是件很無聊的事，但就和生活中許多其他的事情一樣，我們別無選擇。學校離我家很遠，所以我無法走路上學。公車是最經濟又方便的交通工具，所以我一個禮拜有五天得搭公車。如果公車常誤點，就會使人覺得更沮喪。所以我們必須事先想好如何打發等公車時的無聊。

　　爲了應付等車時的無聊，我總是會找些事來做。我常會帶著單字卡研讀英文單字。我的字彙能力也因此大爲進步。如果學校功課不忙的話，我喜歡檢討自己的行爲，看看哪些是好的，哪些有待改進。等公車一來，我就又能做好更充份的準備上學去了。

\*\* ─────────────────────────────

economical〔͵ikə'nɑmɪkḷ〕*adj.* 節省的；經濟的
travel〔'trævḷ〕*v.* 旅行；行進　　***on time*** 準時
frustrating〔'frʌstretɪŋ〕*adj.* 令人沮喪的
boredom〔'bɔrdəm〕*n.* 無聊
fight〔faɪt〕*v.* 設法戰勝　　***bring along*** 帶著…一起
vocabulary〔və'kæbjə͵lɛrɪ〕*n.* 字彙
***in this way*** 如此一來　　improve〔ɪm'pruv〕*v.* 改善
***a great deal*** 大量地；很多
schoolwork〔'skul͵wɝk〕*n.* 功課；學業
examine〔ɪg'zæmɪn〕*v.* 檢查

## ◉ 歷屆大學學測與指考英文作文試題分析 ◉

| 年　度 | 作　文　題　目 | 個人體驗 | 週遭事物 | 說明文 | 敘述文 | 主題句 | 中文敘述 |
|---|---|:-:|:-:|:-:|:-:|:-:|:-:|
| | | 內　容 | | | 文　體 | | |
| 102 學測 | 看圖說故事 | | | | ✓ | | ✓ |
| 102 指考 | 選擇隱形披風或智慧型眼鏡 | | | ✓ | | | ✓ |
| 103 學測 | 看圖說故事 | | | | ✓ | | ✓ |
| 103 指考 | 看圖表，比較自己和美國某高中學生一天的時間分配 | ✓ | | ✓ | | | ✓ |
| 104 學測 | 暑期閱讀：從兩本書中擇一，並說明書中可能的內容及選擇該書的理由 | | | ✓ | | | ✓ |
| 104 指考 | 一次學習或指導他人學習的經驗 | ✓ | | | ✓ | | ✓ |
| 105 學測 | 對家事分工的看法，並描述個人經驗及感想 | ✓ | ✓ | ✓ | ✓ | | ✓ |
| 105 指考 | 「碩士清潔員滿街跑」的原因，你要如何因應，並具體說明你對大學生涯的學習規劃 | ✓ | | ✓ | | | ✓ |
| 106 學測 | 看圖說故事 | | | | ✓ | | ✓ |
| 106 指考 | 說明為何與何時會感到寂寞，並描述某個人、事、物，如何伴你度過寂寞時光 | ✓ | ✓ | ✓ | ✓ | | ✓ |
| 107 學測 | 描述「排隊現象」，並說明自己對此現象的心得與感想 | ✓ | ✓ | ✓ | ✓ | | ✓ |
| 107 指考 | 學校預計舉辦社區活動，方案三選一，敘述活動內容，並說明設計理由 | | | ✓ | | | ✓ |
| 108 學測 | 指出台灣最令人驕傲的二個面向或事物，並說明如何介紹或行銷這些台灣特色 | | ✓ | ✓ | | | ✓ |
| 108 指考 | 看圖表敘述美國青年對各新聞類別的關注度，並說明自己較關注或較不關注的類別及原因 | | | ✓ | | | ✓ |
| 109 學測 | 看圖說故事 | | | | ✓ | | ✓ |
| 109 指考 | 如何維護校園安全 | ✓ | ✓ | | | | ✓ |
| 110 學測 | 看圖說故事 | | | | ✓ | | ✓ |
| 110 指考 | 是否同意教授以英語講授專業課程 | | ✓ | ✓ | | | |
| 111 學測 | 看圖說故事 | | ✓ | | ✓ | | |
| 112 學測 | 說明表情符號（emoji）的溝通功能，及可能造成的誤會或困擾，並提出解決之道 | ✓ | ✓ | ✓ | ✓ | | ✓ |
| 113 學測 | 除了課業壓力之外，青少年常遭遇三個問題，你最想請機器人小幫手幫忙解決哪一個問題，為什麼？並說明你希望這個機器人小幫手具備什麼特質或能力，以及如何和你合作解決問題 | ✓ | ✓ | ✓ | | | ✓ |
| 小　計 | | 11 | 11 | 16 | 12 | 0 | 21 |

★〜〜 **112 年學測英文作文評分要點** 〜〜★

1. 文不對題者，以零分計算。
2. 長度以 120 至 150 個單字（words）為原則，多於 150 字不扣分，少於 120 字酌予扣分。
3. 評分標準：內容 5 分，組織 5 分，文法 4 分，用字遣詞 4 分，拼字、大小寫及標點符號 2 分。
4. 請勿在試卷上留下評閱痕跡，以免影響下位評分教授之評閱。
5. 得分數如為個位數，請勿在其前加上 0 字。例如，5 分只需寫 5，而不必寫 05。
6. 請給整數分數。

說明：1. 依提示在「答案卷」上寫一篇英文作文。
　　　2. 文長至少 120 個單詞（words）。

提示：隨著社群媒體的普及，表情符號（emoji）的使用也極為普遍。請參考下列表情符號，寫一篇英文作文，文分兩段。第一段說明人們何以喜歡使用表情符號，並從下列的表情符號中舉一至二例，說明表情符號在溝通上有何功能。第二段則以個人或親友的經驗為例，討論表情符號在訊息表達或解讀上可能造成的誤會或困擾，並提出可以化解的方法。

《範例》

## Be Careful with Your Emojis

　　We can find emojis in text messages, social media, dating apps and just about anything we can write.　They are very popular because they let people express their emotions easily. *For example*, the smiley emoji can make what we write appear more friendly. And if we use the laughing emoji, our reader can know that we are sharing a joke and are not so serious. *On the other hand*, we can share a negative feeling about something by using the frowning emoji. We can share our disappointment or anger without having to write any negative words.

*However*, emojis can sometimes cause some misunderstandings, especially when we write to people we don't know very well. *Once* my friend made a mistake that was a little embarrassing for her. When she texted me about it, I sent her a laughing emoji. I meant to tell her that it was not so serious and just a funny story that she could laugh about. But she thought I was laughing at her and got mad. To avoid this kind of thing, we should not use emojis when someone is feeling bad. We must be more careful of our friends' feelings. In this situation, writing more words is better. Emojis are easy to use, but it is also easy to be careless with them.

內容 5 分，組織 5 分，文法 4 分，用字遣詞 3 分，大小寫及標點符號 2 分。
⇨總分 19 分

※ 此篇文章非模範作文，是大考中心閱卷老師評分標準的依據及參考文章。

## ★ ～～ 113 年學測英文作文評分要點 ～～★

1. 文不對題者，以零分計算。
2. 長度以 120 至 150 個單字（words）為原則，多於 150 字不扣分，少於 120 字酌予扣分。
3. 評分標準：內容 5 分，組織 5 分，文法 4 分，用字遣詞 4 分，拼字、大小寫及標點符號 2 分。
4. 請勿在試卷上留下評閱痕跡，以免影響下位評分教授之評閱。
5. 得分數如為個位數，請勿在其前加上 0 字。例如，5 分只需寫 5，而不必寫 05。
6. 請給整數分數。

說明： 1. 依提示在「答案卷」上寫一篇英文作文。
　　　 2. 文長至少 120 個單詞（words）。

提示： 這個世代的青少年除了有課業壓力外，生活上也常面對一些困擾與挑戰。下列三張圖分別呈現青少年經常遭遇的三種問題，如果你有一個機器人小幫手可以幫你解決其中一個問題，你會選擇哪一個？請寫一篇英文作文，文分兩段，第一段說明你最想解決哪一個問題，並解釋原因。第二段說明你希望這個機器人小幫手具備什麼特質或能力、可以如何和你分工合作來解決此問題。

《範例》

### My Biggest Problem

　　Like most teenagers, I face many challenges. Aside from my schoolwork, the thing that I find most difficult to deal

deal with is what others think of me. *Of course*, everyone wants to make a good impression and have a good reputation, so what others think of us is important. *However*, I feel that this can go to extremes. I worry too much about what my friends, classmates, and teachers think of me and of everything I do and say. *For example*, I worry about their opinion of my taste in music, the way I speak, even my new haircut. This is not healthy because it gives me stress. *In addition*, being overly concerned about what others think can keep me from doing the things I want to do or taking risks and trying new things.

I would love to have a robot assistant to help me with this problem. This assistant would have to have good analytical skills to help me understand situations and make the right choices for me. It would act like a counselor and listen to me carefully. If I am afraid to try something, it would help me identify the reason. If the reason is only the opinion of others, then it would encourage me to focus on myself. *In short*, this assistant would help me to become my own person.

內容 5 分，組織 5 分，文法 4 分，用字遣詞 3 分，大小寫及標點符號 2 分。
⇨總分 19 分

※ 此篇文章非模範作文，是大考中心閱卷老師評分標準的依據及參考文章。

心得筆記欄

# 跟著百萬網紅「劉毅完美英語」學英文

　　你在捷運上，看到的都是手機。用手機聊天、玩遊戲，都是浪費時間，用手機上「快手」、「抖音」網站，用英文留言，這是心對心的交流，朋友越多，英文越進步。

　　每堂課平均約30秒，每天有2~3堂課，任何時間、任何地點都可以重複練習，在線上從小學、國中、高中、大學到成人，不分年齡、不分程度，人人可學可和劉毅老師一對一討論，什麼問題都可以問，有問必答！用劉毅老師說的話來留言，寫得愈多，進步愈多！可以輕鬆應付任何考試！

→ 立即掃描QR碼，下載「快手」、「抖音」，搜索「劉毅完美英語」，點讚、分享及關注，成為粉絲，享受免費英語課程！

# 劉毅「完美英語系列」

　　不背單字，因為你無法造句。不背一個句子，因為會忘記。要一次背三個短句，能讓你出口成章，句句金句，英文琅琅上口。

　　以前，學英文要查單字字典。現在，想要說什麼，查「完美英語會話寶典」、「完美英語之心靈盛宴」、「英文三字經」、「英文二字經」、「英文一字經」。也可以在「快手」和「抖音」上搜尋「劉毅完美英語」的視頻。例如：你想要查有關Life的句子，你馬上可以在「英文三字經」中查到以下完美的三個句子：

> Life is beautiful. 人生很美。
> Life is sweet. 人生很甜。
> Life is precious. 人生珍貴。

　　人類最可怕的病不是癌症，而是「心病」。劉毅老師的「完美英語」系列叢書，是療癒心靈的最佳良方。

> Perfect English is very healthy.
> 「完美英語」有益健康。
> It's a fountain of youth.
> 是青春之泉。
> It will make you become younger.
> 會使你變得更年輕。

**劉毅「完美英語系列」 每本書/售價990元**

# 易背英作文 100 篇
100 English Compositions
for the College Entrance Exam

定價：150 元

---

編　　　著 / 謝　靜　芳

發　行　所 / 學習出版有限公司　　　☎ (02) 2704-5525

郵 撥 帳 號 / 05127272 學習出版社帳戶

登　記　證 / 局版台業 2179 號

印　刷　所 / 文聯彩色印刷有限公司

台 北 門 市 / 台北市許昌街 17 號 6F　　☎ (02) 2331-4060

台灣總經銷 / 紅螞蟻圖書有限公司　　☎ (02) 2795-3656

本公司網址　www.learnbook.com.tw

電 子 郵 件　learnbook0928@gmail.com

---

2024 年 3 月 1 日新修訂

---

ISBN 978-986-231-156-1

# 高三同學要如何準備「升大學考試」

　　考前該如何準備「學測」呢？「劉毅英文」的同學很簡單，只要熟讀每次的模考試題就行了。每一份試題都在7000字範圍內，就不必再背7000字了，從後面往前複習，越後面越重要，一定要把最後10份試題唸得滾瓜爛熟。根據以往的經驗，詞彙題絕對不會超出7000字範圍。每年題型變化不大，只要針對下面幾個大題準備即可。

### 準備「詞彙題」最佳資料：

背了再背，背到滾瓜爛熟，讓背單字變成樂趣。

### 考前不斷地做模擬試題就對了！

你做的題目愈多，分數就愈高。不要忘記，每次參加模考前，都要背單字、背自己所喜歡的作文。考壞不難過，勇往直前，必可得高分！

練習「模擬試題」，可參考「學習出版公司」最新出版的「7000字學測試題詳解」。我們試題的特色是：
①以「高中常用7000字」為範圍。②經過外籍專家多次校對，不會學錯。③每份試題都有詳細解答，對錯答案均有明確交待。

# 「克漏字」如何答題

第二大題綜合測驗（即「克漏字」），不是考句意，就是考簡單的文法。當四個選項都不相同時，就是考句意，就沒有文法的問題；當四個選項單字相同、字群排列不同時，就是考文法，此時就要注意到文法的分析，大多是考連接詞、分詞構句、時態等。「克漏字」是考生最弱的一環，你難，別人也難，只要考前利用這種答題技巧，勤加練習，就容易勝過別人。

準備「綜合測驗」（克漏字）可參考「學習出版公司」最新出版的「7000字克漏字詳解」。

**本書特色：**
1. 取材自大規模考試，英雄所見略同。
2. 不超出7000字範圍，不會做白工。
3. 每個句子都有文法分析，一目了然。
4. 對錯答案都有明確交待，列出生字，不用查字典。
5. 經過「劉毅英文」同學實際考過，效果極佳。

# 「文意選填」答題技巧

在做「文意選填」的時候，一定要冷靜。你要記住，一個空格一個答案，如果你不知道該選哪個才好，不妨先把詞性正確的選項挑出來，如介詞後面一定是名詞，選項裡面只有兩個名詞，再用刪去法，把不可能的選項刪掉。也要特別注意時間的掌控，已經用過的選項就劃掉，以免重複考慮，浪費時間。

準備「文意選填」，可參考「學習出版公司」最新出版的「7000字文意選填詳解」。

特色與「7000字克漏字詳解」相同，不超出7000字的範圍，有詳細解答。

# 「閱讀測驗」的答題祕訣

① 尋找關鍵字——整篇文章中，最重要就是第一句和最後一句，第一句稱為主題句，最後一句稱為結尾句。每段的第一句和最後一句，第二重要，是該段落的主題句和結尾句。從「主題句」和「結尾句」中，找出相同的關鍵字，就是文章的重點。因為美國人從小被訓練，寫作文要注重主題句，他們給學生一個題目後，要求主題句和結尾句都必須有關鍵字。

② 先看題目、劃線、找出答案、標題號——考試的時候，先把閱讀測驗題目瀏覽一遍，在文章中掃瞄和題幹中相同的關鍵字，把和題目相關的句子，用線畫起來，便可一目了然。通常一句話只會考一題，你畫了線以後，再標上題號，接下來，你找其他題目的答案，就會更快了。

③ 碰到難的單字不要害怕，往往在文章的其他地方，會出現同義字，因為寫文章的人不喜歡重覆，所以才會有難的單字。

④ 如果閱測內容已經知道，像時事等，你就可以直接做答了。

準備「閱讀測驗」，可參考「學習出版公司」最新出版的「7000字閱讀測驗詳解」，本書不超出7000字範圍，每個句子都有文法分析，對錯答案都有明確交待，單字註明級數，不需要再查字典。

# 「中翻英」如何準備

可參考劉毅老師的「英文翻譯句型講座實況DVD」，以及「文法句型180」和「翻譯句型800」。考前不停地練習中翻英，翻完之後，要給外籍老師改。翻譯題做得越多，越熟練。

# 「英文作文」怎樣寫才能得高分？

① 字體要寫整齊，最好是印刷體，工工整整，不要塗改。

② 文章不可離題，尤其是每段的第一句和最後一句，最好要有題目所說的關鍵字。

③ 不要全部用簡單句，句子最好要有各種變化，單句、複句、合句、形容詞片語、分詞構句等，混合使用。

④ 不要忘記多使用轉承語，像 *at present*（現在），*generally speaking*（一般說來），*in other words*（換句話說），*in particular*（特別地），*all in all*（總而言之）等。

⑤ 拿到考題，最好先寫作文，很多同學考試時，作文來不及寫，吃虧很大。但是，如果看到作文題目不會寫，就先寫測驗題，這個時候，可將題目中作文可使用的單字、成語圈起來，寫作文時就有東西寫了。但千萬記住，絕對不可以抄考卷中的句子，一旦被發現，就會以零分計算。

⑥ 試卷有規定標題，就要寫標題。記住，每段一開始，要內縮5或7個字母。

⑦ 可多引用諺語或名言，並注意標點符號的使用。文章中有各種標點符號，會使文章變得更美。

⑧ 整體的美觀也很重要，段落的最後一行字數不能太少，也不能太多。段落的字數要平均分配，不能第一段只有一、兩句，第二段一大堆。第一段可以比第二段少一點。

準備「英文作文」，可參考「學習出版公司」出版的：